"earth did you find daisies?"

She stretched on tiptoes for a quick hug. He smelled of cologne and hair gel. It felt awkward between them.

"Congratulations, short stuff." He quickly walked around the front of the truck and entered the driver's side. "I ordered the daisies through Confetti. They're your fav…" He shook his head, a dismayed look on his face. "They used to be your favorites. Has that changed?"

His question brought a curious sadness to her heart. At one time they had known each other's very thoughts; now uncertainty existed between them.

Despite all that, a strange indefinable feeling of rightness threatened to spiral out of control and cause her to feel good—to feel wanted, to feel…loved. But experience had taught her to be cautious.

Books by Jean Kincaid

Love Inspired Heartsong Presents

The Marriage Ultimatum
A Home in His Heart
Wedding at the Hacienda

JEAN KINCAID

and her husband, Dale, are missionaries to the Hispanic people in Old Mexico and the Rio Grande Valley. Her husband pastors Cornerstone Baptist Church in Donna, Texas, where Jean teaches the junior girls' class and sings in the rondalla. They have three adult children and twelve grandchildren. Jean speaks at ladies' retreats and women's events, and enjoys all things mission related. Her favorite time of day is early morning, when she spends time in devotional reading and prayer. Her heart's desire is to create stories that will draw people to a saving knowledge of our Lord Jesus Christ. You may contact her at www.jeankincaid.com.

JEAN KINCAID

Wedding at
the Hacienda

HEARTSONG
PRESENTS

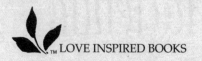 LOVE INSPIRED BOOKS

Recycling programs for this product may not exist in your area.

ISBN-13: 978-0-373-48691-5

WEDDING AT THE HACIENDA

www.Harlequin.com

Printed in U.S.A.

A friend loveth at all times.
—*Proverbs* 17:17

This book is dedicated to
the Wednesday Night Church gang at CBC.
You continually give me fresh ideas for stories.
Also to my girls, Laura, Katelyn, Leah and Tabitha.
I love you to the moon and back.

And in remembrance of my mother, Margie Crump,
and my dear friend Lucille Dowdy.
I lost you both this year but you live on in my heart.

Chapter 1

Raoul Fuentes needed a diversion to make his brothers drop their interrogation. He stood up and said, "Would you newlyweds like something to drink?"

"Yes." His sister-in-law Kayla started to rise.

"Stay put. I'll have Adele bring iced tea." He walked to the French doors of the grand foyer that extended back to the kitchen. Raising his voice to be heard over the chattering in the living room he called, "Adele, bring us five glasses of sweet tea, would you."

"Get it yourself. I'm busy," she hollered from somewhere in the hacienda.

The sudden silence was deafening. He placed a hand on the door frame, seeking support. How he hated to turn around and see the pity on the faces of his family. Couldn't Adele just once in her life behave like one of his sisters-in-law in the room behind him? Carina and Kayla were graceful, well-mannered ladies. And they were Adele's friends. Shouldn't their sweet attitudes rub off on her just a little? Before he could turn, Carina and Kayla passed him, headed to the kitchen. Soon, all he could hear was the delighted screams of Adele welcoming them home, and he could easily imagine the hugging and hand-holding that was sure to take place in the kitchen until every little detail was shared.

He struggled to capture his composure, then turned to find sheepish grins on his brothers' faces. How he itched for one of their brawls where he could work out his frustration in a good old fistfight. And though neither of his brothers would back away from a fight, since they had all become faithful to church he doubted that would be their first choice for settling a family matter. Sure would feel good, though.

Reluctantly he joined them and breathed a sigh of relief when they good-naturedly slapped him on the back and said, "Women," as if that explained away Adele's bad attitude.

Raoul's relief was short-lived, though, because they started in on the plantation again. If they hadn't bailed him out of several scrapes already, he'd tell them where to get off, that they had their own businesses to run and that he could handle the Citrus Queen without their interference. But for now he would put their worries to rest.

"I have reason to believe this will be the greatest grapefruit harvest the Citrus Queen has had in several years. If it will slow up on the rain, things should turn around come September."

Juan Antonio, the middle brother, clapped him on the shoulder. "Now, that's good to hear."

"Raoul, what's all the secrecy about?" Marcelo, the oldest of his brothers, could never take anything at face value. He dug and dug until he got the answers he wanted. "Adele says you tried something new but she has no clue what. You rob a bank or something? How'd you get the funding?"

Raoul felt exasperated every time his brothers meddled in his affairs. They weren't part of the operations at The Queen anymore, though they still owned stock. But even if they didn't own stock, they were family, and that counted even more in the Fuentes way of thinking. However, just once in his life he wished they would let him be until he could prove himself. "No funding required—just a lot of studying and experimenting. And nothing to report till the first grapefruit is tasted, so no worries, brother. We still have plenty of the Reds should the new fruit not work out."

"So, what kind of experiments?" Marcelo sat on the edge of an end table, so Raoul knew he was settling in for the long haul. He would have to clue his brothers in. He'd be lying if he didn't feel a bit of pride in what he had to reveal, but he wished it could have been later on in the year when he might have something to show for his hard work.

"Remember two years ago, when Juan Antonio went to Mexico to sell Grampa's place, and you were building your ranch? Well, we harvested the first grapefruits off the orchards I planted when I first inherited The Queen. You guys remember, right? When I planted the back sixty acres with rootstock and grafted in a new budwood variety?" At their nods, he continued. "The harvest was a failure. The fruit was pithy and not edible, but now, oh, my soul, we cut one open in the March harvest and it was sweeter than our Reds." Excitement caused Raoul to speak too loudly, so he lowered his voice. "It still had tartness, though, and after tasting several from different trees we sent samples to our buyers. Every company has ordered a truckload along with the Rios. If they follow through, we will have double, possibly even triple the normal business."

"And once word gets out, sales will double here in the Rio Grande Valley, as well." Juan Antonio's smile broadened in approval.

"You're gonna need more manpower during harvest and that will cut into your profits." Always the thorough one, Marcelo covered every angle. He paced a few feet, then stood motionless in the middle of the room. Raoul remained silent, knowing his brother would come up with a plan. That was okay with him, but he already had things worked out in his own mind. He didn't have long to wait for Marcelo's plan. "I'll bring my men and Juan Antonio can bring his and we'll knock harvest out in a few weeks."

Juan Antonio, ever the peacemaker, seemed to instinctively know that Raoul wanted to work things out for himself. "Well, we have until September. A lot can happen during that time." Raoul *almost* relaxed when he saw the satisfied smile on his brother's face. "Good job, Raoul." *Almost.* "Who'd a thought our little play-boy brother could be so smart? When you going to tell Adele so she can stop thinking you're a lazy bum?"

"Keep this quiet, please. I'd like to stay one step ahead of the other Valley growers. Competition is tough because of the economy."

"And Adele?" Marcelo's eyes were interested and contemplative. "It might take a lot of stress off her to know there is light at the end of the tunnel."

"More important, it might make her like you again." Juan Antonio stared at him then burst out laughing. "Well, it won't hurt. Could, possibly, gain you a few brownie points."

"Not interested, and Adele is the last person I plan to tell. She'd find something to complain about just to make my life miserable." Raoul knew the second the words left his mouth that she was behind him. The arrested expressions on his brothers' faces and Marcelo's taut head jerk spoke louder than words. He turned to look and Adele's face was crimson with resentment and humiliation. Raoul's embarrassment at being overheard quickly turned to annoyance. She could sass and constantly put him down in public but he wasn't allowed to criticize her to his family? She could get over it. "Speak of the devil." He knew he shouldn't have said it, but it seemed he'd taken leave of his senses.

"What are you not telling me, Raoul?" The cold edge of accusation in her voice snapped the last nerve of his patience. First his brothers' well-meaning but determined questioning and now Adele, who was not even family, thought she needed to know his business. "I'd like to know what I'm going to be up against. Because we both know I'll be the one picking up the pieces."

Raoul suppressed his anger under the appearance of indifference. "Poor Della. So overworked and underappreciated."

"All right, you two. Go to your respective corners." Carina, Juan Antonio's wife, wasn't having any of it. "Think happy thoughts." She settled on the sofa, one leg underneath and patted the seat beside her. "Come, Kayla, tell us more about New York. What did Marcelo think of the Empire State Building?"

Raoul returned Adele's glowering look with a sardonic expression he could tell sent her temper soaring. So be it. The kid gloves were off. He was through protecting his childhood friend. She was graduating from college for goodness' sake. It was time she stood on her own two feet and if that meant she had to move out of his home, the only home she'd known since she was six, then so be it. It wasn't as though he had committed to taking care of her for life. He rubbed his stomach. Why did thoughts of Adele always give him indigestion?

Adele reined in her thoughts and focused on the laptop screen in front of her. Two more exams and she'd be finished with four long years of college. But the reward would be that diploma stating she had a degree in business. She clicked Finished on the first test then pulled up the next battery of questions. She scrolled to the bottom. Okay, so fifty questions. Piece of cake. Right. And she held the deed to The Queen. In her dreams.

Forty-five minutes later she clicked Send to her professor's email, shut her laptop and stood wearily to her feet. She had an hour before she had to be at the convention center to practice the graduation exercise, so she headed to the Mexican café close by. She ordered a celebratory fajita *botana* platter for one; might as well celebrate alone because no one else cared if she finished or not. Her dad would be proud of her, but it hadn't been his wish for her to get a business degree. He wanted something easier; how *had* he said it...more feminine? And Raoul knew she'd studied religiously every evening, but even he'd shown no interest nor asked any questions, even when he'd caught her crying over a term paper.

She dug in with a hearty appetite, relief lending a hand to her hunger. No more studying, reading huge books that required page after page of problem solving, computer exercises, graphs and Excel spreadsheets. The five hours she spent in school each day could now be put to work in the office at the Citrus Queen.

When they'd been kids, Raoul, Juan Antonio, Marcelo and she herself had dubbed the plantation The Queen rather than the Citrus Queen. It stuck and before long the entire family called it that. Times had been happier then. She'd tagged along behind the boys in every scrape. They swam in the arroyo, fished together and played among the rows of grapefruit trees from early sunup until sundown. As Marcelo and Juan Antonio grew older they began to devise ways to hide from her. But even if Raoul joined his brothers, he eventually returned to be with her. Their friendship had been solid, unshakable.

Only after they'd graduated from high school and Raoul had taken on responsibility for the plantation had things changed. He'd gone on overnight trips to sign new clients and the traveling bug had enticed him into more and more trips. Leisure trips not connected to business at all. He'd taken to staying out late at night and even though he was up and out early the next morning she had no idea where he went. But she felt certain it wasn't to work in the orchards because the financial side of the business kept dwindling and his trips did not help matters one bit.

When she tried to talk to him about it he became defensive and refused to discuss his whereabouts with her. Most often she felt like his mother rather than his friend. And when his mother actually moved to the east coast, the responsibility for Raoul landed even more heavily on her shoulders. But what could she do? She'd been rescuing him from trouble since they were seven.

"Is this seat taken?" Adele glanced up into eyes so vivid blue she immediately thought of the ocean off the coast of Mazatlan.

"Not at all. Please, have a seat." She moved the chip basket closer to her side of the table, making room for his tray and drink. He extended his hand and she was impressed at the firm grasp as they shook.

"Daniel Jacobs," he introduced himself, "and you are Adele Rivas, graduating business class." He grinned at her raised eyebrows. "Yes, my sitting here is deliberate. I have a business proposition for you." He placed a napkin across his lap and Adele took the chance to study his features. Short blond hair with smooth shaven face, strong jawline and straight white teeth that he revealed as he smiled at her. She felt a hint of blush creep into her cheeks as her eyes returned to his. This man was almost too handsome for his own good.

"I promise I'm a good guy and you have the freedom to tell me to get lost if you don't like what I'm suggesting."

"And I have no problem telling you exactly that. If you don't mind I need you to hurry because I have an appointment elsewhere."

"Yes, I know. The convention center for graduation exercises. I'm on the board there." He took a drink of his tea and grimaced. "Unsweet. I specifically asked for sweet tea." He opened a packet of sweetener and added it before he spoke again. "I'm told that you are graduating with honors. Very impressive. I'm looking for someone to streamline my business. My records are a mess and the state issued a mandate that I either fix that little problem or close down."

"What do you do?"

"I'm a large animal vet and I just signed a contract to work through the state wildlife department. The state may randomly inspect at any time, so records have to be kept up-to-date and the financial end of things must be aboveboard and current." He ate quickly, allowing her time to think through what he'd said.

"Why me?"

"The main reason is because you're my neighbor and can get to my place in minutes, and secondly, because you're the best according to one of your professors who also serves on the convention center board." He smiled at her and she found herself comparing him to Raoul. So very different yet both men were stunningly handsome. This one, though, had a good work ethic to back him up. Something Adele found very enticing.

She remembered the Fuentes brothers had discussed renting one of their buildings on the frontage road of the property. So this was the new renter who had saved the day for them. The deposit and first month's rent had gone to pay retirement benefits on the employees of The Queen. She'd wondered how they would pay the bill, and had prayed a prayer of thanks that once again God had met the need.

"I don't see how I can help you." She might as well get this over with. "My dad is the manager, but he retires from the Citrus Queen the day they hand me my diploma. I take over the entire business end of the plantation." *That is if Raoul doesn't fire me and I can make it productive,* she thought to herself. "It's a full-time job." At least to get her plans in motion it would be.

He studied her a moment, then looked down at his plate. He seemed to ponder his next words. Finally he looked up and seemed to reach a decision. "The work I need you to do, organizing the records and setting up files and so on, can be done at the Citrus Queen if you'd rather not leave. It's basic bookkeeping and file making. Once things are organized, I'm thinking fifteen to twenty hours a week will be all that's required to maintain the system."

She could actually draw a salary. The thought sent waves of excitement through her. Her mind raced through possibilities. With the extra cash flow poured into The Queen's many delinquent accounts, she just might meet her self-imposed deadline by the year's end. A slender thread of hope began to weave its way through her. She came to a quick decision.

"I graduate next week on…"

"June 23, I know." Amusement flickered in the eyes that met hers. "The big day."

Adele couldn't help the smile that tipped up the corners of her mouth. It felt good to have someone recognize the specialness of her graduation. "Right. I'm rehearsing for graduation today and tomorrow, then after graduation I'm vacationing for a week. I can start working for you the week after the Fourth of July if that's acceptable." She'd had no plans for a vacation but Raoul's hurtful words lingered in the recesses of her mind and just maybe it would do her good to get away. Relax a few days before she devoted a year of her precious time to saving her home. And the week of the fourth was crammed with family events and celebrations she had no intention of missing.

"It's a deal." They shook hands again and Adele excused herself. The day suddenly seemed a lot brighter.

Chapter 2

Three days later she stood in the recesses of the wide corridor surrounding the main reception room of the convention center. Her heart beat a mile a minute as she heard the processional march begin for the graduates to enter. She followed single file and remained standing until three hundred students filled the seats around her. Her heart swelled with pride at her accomplishment but loneliness threatened to steal her joy. She had asked for only one seat and had given just one invitation to this event. She'd given it to her dad. She didn't really expect him to be there, he hated crowds, but she'd thought maybe he should be notified of her accomplishment. She hadn't known whether Marcelo and Kayla would be back from their honeymoon, and Juan Antonio and

Carina had date night on Friday nights so she hadn't invited them. And Lord only knew where Raoul would be.

She clued back into the ceremony when the students around her stood. They placed their tassels on the other side of their caps and began the exit march. Pandemonium could only describe the next fifteen minutes. She'd almost made it to the outside door when she was hauled back against a broad chest and lifted in a bear hug. Her feet left the floor and she started giggling. It might help if she could see who held her. Once her feet touched the floor again she turned, congratulations ready for a fellow student, only to find Raoul. Caught off guard she looked at him in surprise, remembering vividly his hostility from just a week ago.

"Raoul, what are you doing here?"

He shrugged matter-of-factly. "We've shared every major milestone of our lives together. I couldn't see letting this one pass and not celebrating with you." The expression in his currant-black eyes seemed to plead for friendship; for a truce. She stared, momentarily speechless in surprise. They hadn't been on the same page for several years now. His many mistakes and failed endeavors haunted her; like an old wound that ached on a rainy day. Did she even want to share her special day with him? Was it possible to celebrate with someone who continually let you down? Something flickered in the eyes that held hers; disappointment maybe, at her hesitation.

She took a deep breath, praying she wasn't making the biggest mistake of her life. "Okay, then. Let's get out of here and celebrate. I never want to see the inside of a classroom again."

She couldn't help but notice he seemed very pleased with himself. He took her hand and determinedly cut a path through the swarms of people inside and outside the building until they arrived at his truck. He opened her door and reached for something on the seat. He turned to her with a huge bouquet of daisies. She caught her breath, misgivings increasing by the minute. A sense of inadequacy swept over her. How was she supposed to react? Was this the time to let bygones be bygones? Could she forget the past four years of bickering, hostilities and accusations? She held the flowers to her nose, sniffing their aroma, hiding her thoughts, unwilling to face him yet unable to turn away, concerned by the overwhelming desire to share this special evening with someone familiar, and to find gratification over her hard work.

She came to a decision, praying it was the right one. Loneliness and confusion were her constant companions and her future looked bleak, but tonight she would celebrate a good meal with a friend. What could it hurt? Somehow that thought didn't quiet the conflicting emotions in her mind.

"Raoul, these are beautiful. Where on earth did you find daisies?" She stretched on tiptoes for a quick hug. He smelled of cologne and hair gel. It felt awkward between them.

"Congratulations, short stuff." He quickly walked around the front of the truck and entered the driver's side. "I ordered the daisies through Confetti. They're your fav…" He shook his head, a dismayed look on his face. "They used to be your favorites. Has that changed?"

His question brought a curious sadness to her heart. At one time they had known each other's very thoughts; now uncertainty existed between them.

"Daisies are still my favorites." She laid them across her lap and buckled her seat belt. "Wait, Raoul. What about my car?"

He looked at her in smug delight. "Your dad rode with me and he took your car back to The Queen."

"My dad was here?" Shock caused her voice to rise. Her dad rarely left home and he certainly would not be comfortable in a large crowd.

"Of course. Did you really think he'd miss his only daughter's graduation from college?"

Her mind whirled. She turned to Raoul as he placed his keys in the ignition. "Why didn't he wait to see me?" A strange indefinable feeling of rightness threatened to spiral out of control and cause her to feel good; to feel wanted, to feel…loved. But experience had taught her to be cautious.

"As soon as the class stood for the tassel change he hightailed it out of there, sweating profusely." When Raoul smiled he seemed ten years younger. Her sense of humor took over and she brought her hand up to stifle her giggles. "I think he had visions of actually having to smile and talk to people." He faked a shudder, then burst out laughing.

"We should have made him get out more over the years." She thought of the many times she'd begged him to go with her to Padre Island. Or just to run out to the local ice cream parlor. Occasionally he'd given in and taken her but he'd always stayed in the vehicle.

"Yeah we should have but it became easier to leave him behind. He was content and we were happy not to have to keep begging him."

They rode in silence for a while, both in deep contemplation. When they started up the long drive to the hacienda she became instantly wide-awake. "Hey," she exclaimed, her body stiffening. "I thought we were celebrating."

"We will. I just need to get something I left in the house. I won't be but a second. Do you need to check on anything?"

"I'd like to put these in water. I'll do it right quick."

"Sounds good." He pocketed his keys and they climbed the steps to the front door. Like the gentleman she knew he could be he opened the door for her.

"Surprise." Voices yelled at her as she stepped into the house. Caught off guard she fell back against Raoul and his arm tightened across her shoulders. Carina and Kayla crowded round for a hug, and her dad, looking for all the world as if he'd lost his best friend, handed her a badly wrapped gift, then gave her a one-arm hug. Juan Antonio buzzed her cheek with a near kiss and Marcelo patted her on the head. She'd quit trying to make him stop this practice, because her complaints just made it worse. Being five feet four inches to his six-two seemed to supply him with numerous jokes about short people. She knew he loved her, though, because he always took her side.

Alma, the young woman who ran Confetti with Kayla, rescued the daisies from her arms and went in search of a vase. Carina pulled Adele to one of the wing-back chairs in front of the fireplace and began to hand her presents. She looked around the room for Raoul. "You knew about this, didn't you?"

The tenderness in his expression amazed her. He did nothing more than nod but she felt a slender, delicate thread begin to form. For the next hour she became caught up in well wishes, presents and such good food she actually patted her stomach. The kindness and love of her friends sent her spirits soaring and even her walk had a sunny cheerfulness.

As the party was winding down, she picked up several glasses and headed to the kitchen. Alma had placed the daisies in a vase on a sofa table in the foyer along the stair wall. She stopped to admire them and then paused outside the study door. Glancing inside, she saw the Fuentes brothers and her dad, obviously in a serious discussion. Raoul's back was to her and she could tell he was agitated. He stood with feet spread wide apart, hands clenched behind his back. He spoke with quiet firmness. It took her a minute to understand what he said. She bit her lip to stifle the outcry.

"If the Citrus Queen finances have not improved by this time next year, I'm selling this monstrosity and downsizing the orchards to a manageable size and counting my losses."

One of the glasses slipped. She fumbled for it but it hit the tile floor and shattered into a million pieces. Much like her heart. All eyes in the room focused on her and she bent to pick up the shards of glass. Raoul knelt in front of her and caught her hand. "You'll cut yourself."

Humiliation at how naive she'd been and fury at herself for mistakenly believing they could revive their friendship caused her to lash out vehemently. "As if you care whether I'm hurt or not."

She heard his quick intake of breath and his black eyes widened in astonishment. She didn't wait to hear his reply. She stood and looked each of the men in the eyes, staring longest at her dad. It seemed he'd sold her down the drain, too, because she had seen his nod of agreement right as the glass had slipped. Raising her chin she turned and walked from the study, climbed the stairs wearily and went to her room. She dragged her suitcase from under the bed and began to pack. She had to get away. She snuck down the back stairs, skirted the terrace and quietly started her car.

She could see into the drawing room; everyone still laughed and talked. She stared at the mural of the mango plantation in Mexico that covered the entire back wall. The place the mural depicted had been in the Fuentes family for generations and had been handed down to Juan Antonio. Her gaze then lovingly traced the outside lines of her beloved Queen. Everyone had an inheritance but her. She was not family, not blood. She needed time to accept the fact that she could very well lose all that was dear to her heart.

"What did you say?" Raoul tried to disguise his annoyance in front of Adele's dad. Why on earth would

Adele take a vacation the very week he had clients arriving from Alaska?

"She's gone, Jefe. She's celebrating."

"Celebrating what?" He ground out the words impatiently.

"Graduation." Raoul thought he heard a vague hint of disapproval in Joe Rivas's voice. He experienced a gamut of perplexing emotions. First and foremost a sense of overpowering guilt hit him in the solar plexus.

His thoughts winged back to the conversation with her dad the week before Adele's graduation. He hadn't even realized she would graduate this year. What kind of friend was he? "When does she graduate?" he'd asked her dad. As far as he knew, he'd not received an invitation to her graduation. What did that mean? That she didn't want him there? Was it not a big event when someone graduated from college? *Of course it is, you dodo brain,* a tiny voice accused.

"Not this coming Tuesday but next."

"Did she give you an invitation?"

"Yes, didn't you get one?" As their eyes met, Raoul felt a shock run through him.

"Actually, no, she didn't." The look of surprise on Joe's face echoed the confusion in Raoul's soul. He found it very disturbing. Above all else, he'd thought he and Adele were still close friends.

Yet he stood here trying to digest the information that she had gone on vacation without telling him. First no invitation to her graduation and now this. "I can't believe she didn't mention it."

"Guess she forgot." Joe shrugged matter-of-factly

and walked from the room. He returned a moment later with several hundred-dollar bills and tossed them onto the table. "That's for the client meals tonight. Adele will settle with the hotel when she gets back. Use your card for anything else that's needed." His footsteps disappeared down the hall and Raoul stared after him. For some reason he got the distinct impression the man was upset with him. It ran in the family.

He sank into the desk chair behind him. He remembered the look of betrayal in Adele's eyes the night she'd heard them talking in this very study. It appeared the entire Rivas family had something against him. He'd be lying if he said it didn't wear on his nerves. Joe Rivas had been more of a father to him than his own had ever been and Joe's daughter had been the only friend that stuck with him through thick and thin. He knew he had hurt Adele and by so doing he had hurt his mentor and friend. And all over a crazy house that was falling down around their ears.

Slightly more than an hour later he greeted three men from the great state of Alaska and began the long and often boring spiel of haggling over shipping prices to such a distant area. He knew the possibilities were limited and chances were slim to none but The Queen hung on right now by a thread. They had four climate controlled trucks and gas wasn't getting any cheaper. He'd done his homework and reducing costs was not an option.

After a good meal and a walk on the beach he hoped negotiations would be to his benefit. He desperately needed to pull off a few new deals, but he couldn't lose money just to secure a buyer. It had taken him a while to figure out how to put together a business deal. He wasn't a business expert by any means, but he'd finally realized if he didn't protect his investments no one else would. Except Adele. She fought like a tigress to keep their heads above water. But in the long run he feared it might not make any difference. Some days, he didn't hold out much hope for the future of the once-grand Citrus Queen; other days he saw a glimmer of light at the end of the tunnel. He hoped it wasn't a train coming at them.

He'd put the visitors up at a hotel on South Padre Island, another business technique he'd learned from Adele's dad. "Entertain them with good food, conversation and a good night's sleep and you've won half the battle. Ocean air doesn't hurt," he'd said. So a night at the beach was as different an approach as he could manage for someone who spent months on end in the snow. How he hoped it would work.

He bid his guest good night and walked wearily to the elevator doors. He simply wanted to fall into bed and sleep, blessed sweet sleep, then finalize this deal over breakfast. He had a standing invitation to a free room at the hotel, thanks to an old friend of his dad's, and occasionally he took advantage of it. It was merely a case of I'll rub your back if you rub mine. He for sure provided his dad's friend with lots of customers.

At the elevator, he turned and looked back into the restaurant he'd just left. An irritating twitch between his shoulder blades warned him of something. But what? He didn't see anyone; no one hid behind the shrubs and trees elegantly situated in the foyer. The doors swished open and he stepped inside, on guard against whatever was causing the feeling of being watched. But he arrived safely at his room and soon fell into a deep sleep where Adele's sweet laughter soothed away all his worries. He awoke with the certainty that he could never be satisfied with only a dream.

Chapter 3

Adele leaned back on her elbows and squinted up at the sun. The waves lapped at her feet and she sighed. She'd needed this. Seagulls called to each other and swooped down for food. She stuck her toe into the white foam salt water as it came farther into shore. Not many people on the beach today. In another week or so it would be overcrowded. South Padre Island had been a favorite haunt of her and Raoul's during junior high and high school. They would beg a ride from Marcelo or Juan Antonio early in the morning and not return home until late in the evening. Most often when someone remembered where they were and came and got them. She sighed. Those had been the good old days.

A cloud blotted out the sun for a second. It had been that way most of the morning and she knew she was in danger of being sunburned. But she hated to move. This was the life of Riley. She checked the time on her cell phone and reluctantly gathered her things. Book, beach towel, paper and pen. She'd outlined several ways to save or add to the Queen's dwindling coffers. Small pack of tissues. The crying jags were less frequent now, but she never knew when a tiny one might sneak up on her.

She could not quite resign herself to moving out of The Queen, nor could she give up on it totally, but she had accepted the sad truth that she very well could be fighting a losing battle. It really hit home that she did not have a voice in the final decision. One thing, though, when it was over she'd know she had done her best.

At least she had a job to go to. As she trudged over the hot sand to the sidewalk of her hotel she considered the man who had offered her that job. Daniel Jacobs. He was easy on the eyes and single. Her heart skipped a little beat and she stopped in her tracks. What in the world was wrong with her? She had no time for a relationship. But he had a super job and served on important local community boards. And if she was not mistaken, he was only a few years older than her. What more could a woman ask for?

She paused by the pool simply to enjoy looking at the blue water. It was huge, and at the south end water slipped over a fake red rock waterfall. It splashed down into the pool and several kids shrieked as they dove under the stream. Shrubbery surrounded the rocks and made it look like something from the rain forest. The dark green grass surrounding the pool and between the palm trees looked soft enough to sleep on, and the breeze from the ocean made her want to never leave. She had needed this time away. Now hopefully she had her head on straight.

Hours later, showered and rested, she took the elevator down to the lobby and entered the hotel café. Her run this morning and time spent soul-searching while on the beach had made her ravenous. The café provided inside and outside seating and she chose the latter. She placed her order and smiled at the waiter when he brought her lemon water. The sun's last rays filtered over the water, creating a rosy hue, and then it sank like a stone, bringing with it the dusk and loneliness so intense she felt tears threaten. She drew a deep breath and forbade herself to cry.

From her vantage point on the deck overlooking the ocean, Adele watched a group of businessmen enter the restaurant from the hotel foyer. She squinted in the dismal lighting. One of the men looked familiar and if she didn't miss her guess, Raoul Fuentes and she were on Padre Island at the same time and place. What were the chances of that happening? She reached for her glasses, the beach breeze not exactly comfortable for wearing contacts, and knocked her glass of water over. The waiter rushed to offer his help, drawing unwanted attention to her table. She grabbed the menu and held it fully in front of her, all the while assuring the man that things were okay and apologizing for being such a klutz.

Finally, she got the nerve to peek, and sure enough Raoul sat barely fifteen feet away with his back to her, facing the men he was apparently entertaining. One of

the men was older, nearing his sixties she guessed, and
the other two in their early forties. They were laughing
courteously with each other so she figured they weren't
fast friends. What was Raoul doing with them? They
didn't look like grapefruit buyers and she'd made no
dinner appointments for clients for this week. Had he
figured out a way to make money on the side? Illegal
activities of some sort? Surely not. She needed to hear
the conversation at that table, but she didn't want to
alert Raoul to her presence.

She took the menu and glass of water to the inside
section of the restaurant where they sat. The waiter followed behind her with the bread basket and her cutlery
setup. She frowned at him, hoping he'd get the message
and go away. No such luck. "Would the senorita like
to order now?"

A noisy party entered the restaurant so she took the
opportunity to order, confident her voice would not
be heard by the occupants at Raoul's table. But as the
waiter left, she realized her predicament still existed.
Her five feet four inches never drew much attention,
especially around Carina and Kayla—lovingly dubbed
"Amazon women" by Adele—so she bent over to min-
imize herself even more and slipped to the table right
behind Raoul's shoulder. The men didn't even spare
her a glance but as she settled into her chair she looked
up into the eyes of the waiter. He tilted his brow and
looked at her uncertainly. Without blinking, he picked
up her bread basket and cutlery and brought it to her
new table. "Is this table satisfactory for the senorita?"
he inquired sarcastically.

"Shh." She waved him away impatiently. Man, it was hard to get good service these days. As he left with an affronted frown she leaned backward, listening to the conversation behind her. But it couldn't be. With her own ears she heard Raoul explain the cost and effect of shipping grapefruit. She grudgingly admitted it was a good pitch. His facts were dead-on. Amazing. But he'd mentioned nothing about having a meeting tonight and she usually had to book the parties a week or two in advance. Why hadn't he said anything?

She clued back in on the conversation and jumped in surprise. Raoul stood up to answer a phone call, claiming better reception on the outside deck. He would have to pass right by her. She was so busted. Her stomach clenched tight and momentary panic surged through her. She dropped her napkin on the opposite side of her table away from Raoul and in the semidarkness went down on all fours to get it. She crawled a few feet, saw an opening between two tables and kept crawling.

She'd almost rounded the corner out of sight when she bumped headfirst into two legs. Her heart jolted and her pulse pounded in her ears. Intensely humiliated, she sought for an explanation for Raoul. Her gaze travelled up, up, up into the silent gaze of the waiter. Then he knelt in front of her. "Ma'am, I'm afraid we're going to have to ask you to leave." He handed her a black leather folder with her bill tucked nicely inside and a to-go box in a bag touting the restaurant's logo. He walked away and as she stood and slipped that final few feet out of sight behind the wall partition, he returned with her purse. She put the correct amount into the folder with a nice-sized tip, then with as distinguished a look as she could manage, she pointed and mentioned that the table over there needed tea.

She exited the restaurant, dodging from one potted palm to another, finally stopping in a darkened corner of the foyer to see if Raoul just happened to be staying in the same hotel as she. With a dazed exasperation she wondered briefly what had happened to her common sense.

In her room she sank onto the bed and contemplated the meaning of what she'd just witnessed. Most of the time, they entertained clients at the hacienda or in McAllen at a restaurant near Kayla's store, Confetti. The many times she had cooked for clients, her dad had done most of the talking and buyers instinctively trusted him over the youngest Fuentes son who often seemed bored with business transactions. Marcelo and Juan Antonio also brought clients and assured them their investments were safe, but this was the first time she'd seen Raoul handle a business deal on his own. She grudgingly admitted it had been exciting to see Raoul in business mode. His pitch had been nigh on to perfect. Could it be possible that he wanted The Queen to succeed?

Disconcerted she crossed her arms and stared at the floor. Why had he said he would sell if finances didn't turn around for The Queen, then try and find buyers? She had thought he was giving up. Now it looked as though he was working to keep it afloat. So which was it? She was totally bewildered by his behavior.

Her future looked vague and shadowy, just like the

year her mother died. She'd been six years old and had arrived home on the school bus to find an ambulance team working over her mother, who had miscarried and hemorrhaged to death. Blood had been everywhere and her dad sat with his head in his hands, weeping out loud.

Adele had lost two parents that day, because the laughing, happy man who'd been her father retreated into a shell, and though he'd cared for her and met her needs, there'd been no spontaneity in their lives, no sharing emotions and few words of love.

A year later they'd moved into the hacienda. At the time, Raoul's dad had moved back to Mexico to care for the family mango plantation. Raoul's mother, Marta Fuentes, had inherited The Queen and thousands of acres from her side of the family. With her husband in Mexico, she needed a manager for The Queen and Adele and her father needed a new start.

Raoul had been her salvation; Juan Antonio and Marcello had included her like a younger sister and Mrs. Fuentes did what she could to teach Adele things a mother would have taught her.

This had been her home for most of her life. Now it was being threatened, and the sad thing was the threat came from the inside, not the outside. She swallowed hard and bit back tears. She had a year.

Raoul awoke early the next morning, refreshed and ready to meet the day. He savored the feeling of satisfaction that a job well done could bring. Even if he lost the deal, he'd been prepared and he'd not wavered in what he presented to his potential clients. He crossed to the window, eager to see the ocean waters crashing against the sandy beach. The sun had just begun to streak the sky with pink rays and a few people were stirring.

A lone runner jogged along the edge of the water and an old man set his fishing pole firmly in the sand, then sat in a beach chair and stared after the jogger. A twinkle of sunlight caught the black bouncing curls and Raoul chuckled to himself. No wonder the old man stared. The woman was dressed in shorts and a hoodie with a pink iPod belted to her waist and headphones in her ears. Now he knew the cause of the twitching between his shoulder blades. He wondered where Adele had been watching from last night.

Frustration gnawed at him. How he'd love to go down and chase her into the water, like they'd done as kids. Playing until they were too tired to eat their evening meal. But he had breakfast with clients to get through and by then she'd have disappeared. He stared down at her, missing his friend, longing for the companionship they'd once enjoyed, and wishing fervently he could erase the constant worried look she'd worn since high school graduation. No one so young should have to carry such a heavy load. And no one so beautiful should age early because of stress and unhappiness.

She stopped and bent over, hands grasping her thighs. He watched, ready to run to her if she were in distress, but she wiped her brow with the bottom of her hoodie and walked slowly toward the entrance to his hotel. He laughed aloud. Life was good.

A couple of hours later he bid the Alaskan family goodbye, hurried to his room and stashed his briefcase with a freshly signed contract inside. Then he set out to find Adele.

He asked his dad's friend to check and see if she was in her room. She wasn't. He made inquiries and someone remembered they'd seen her shopping on the front streets. He took off at a run.

Looking through the window of a store, he found her. She stood in front of a wall of signs with funny and unique sayings, and she laughed. He watched the happy play of emotions cross her face as she read the more outrageous ones. This is how she should be all the time, he thought. This was the Della from their childhood. Happy, carefree and loving him fiercely.

They had always been inseparable. Now the gulf was too wide to cross—especially since she'd overheard his plan to sell out if things didn't improve. Preoccupied with his thoughts it took him a moment to return to reality. She raised her chin with a cool stare in his direction.

Oh, no, you don't, he muttered under his breath. She turned back to read the plaques but her smile was bleak and tight-lipped. He entered the store and stood beside her, unsure and feeling like a schoolboy. He began to read the signs and before long he couldn't hold back the laughter. Out of the tail of his eye, he saw her lips twitch and he felt a joyous satisfaction.

After a few moments she walked away to look through the T-shirts. He followed. She moved on and he walked with her. They exited the store without purchasing anything but when they passed an ice cream parlor it was more than either of them could resist. As he stepped up to order for them, her smile broadened in approval. Raoul felt as if his dormant wits had renewed themselves. They sat at the tall table in the front window of the store. At one time they would have swapped cones to share the different tastes, but neither of them offered and they remained silent.

"What are you doing here, Raoul?"

Startled at the sound of her voice he took a moment to answer.

"I had clients from Alaska. They wanted to see the ocean so I picked them up at the Brownsville Airport and brought them here. And guess what?"

"What?"

Raoul was barely able to control his joy that they were speaking with no trace of the anger that had been between them for what seemed like years now. "I have a signed contract and earnest money. The check is enough to buy at least one piece of new equipment and do a few repairs."

A soft gasp escaped her. Excitement added shine to her dark eyes and a blush to her cheeks. "For real, Raoul?" At his nod she shrieked, then hastily covered her mouth with a napkin. "Then you won't have to sell The Queen at the end of the year."

So they were back to that. How could anyone be so crazy over brick and mortar? For goodness' sake, it wasn't even hers.

"Della, would it be so bad to live in a new house and not have to stuff papers around the windows in the wintertime? Don't you get tired just trying to hold that place together?" He could hear the anger rising in his tone and lowered his voice deliberately. "Have you even considered the possibility that life would be easier on all of us if we weren't so bogged down with running that monstrosity of a house? That we could make a decent living on the orchards if we didn't have the expense of the hacienda?"

Guilt flooded him when she winced at his words. He pretended not to see. "There comes a time when a person must desert a sinking ship."

She lifted her chin and met his gaze straight on. "One minute you're working to save the place, the next you're preparing to desert. That's the story of your life, Raoul." Every curve of her body spoke defiance. "Have you ever considered," she mimicked his words, "choosing a course and sticking with it?"

Suddenly he could take it no more. He stood and tossed his napkin basketball-style into the nearby trash can. Then he placed a hand on the table and one on the back of her chair. Looking into her beautiful dark eyes he almost wavered but he hardened his heart and delivered a much-needed home truth.

"Here's something for *you* to consider, Della. I can't stick to one course because I have to always consider what will happen to you. But make no mistake, as the owner of the hacienda, I will make the final decision."

Her black eyes darkened with confusion. Her mouth opened in dismay. If that wasn't enough to put a knife in his gut, her eyes filled with tears. He walked away the victor of their argument, but strangely it tasted like gall.

Chapter 4

Adele picked up another potato and unwittingly kept one long continuous peel until the skin broke and fell to the mountain of peelings already on the countertop. It was a monotonous job but one that let her mind wander aimlessly. Tomorrow was the Fourth of July and the family would celebrate at the hacienda all day. Then in the evening they'd pile into the Queen's minibus and drive to South Padre Island for the fireworks out in the bay. This year several new friends would join them for the late-afternoon meal and possibly accompany them to the evening's festivities.

The clothes dryer buzzed, so she washed her hands and hurried to the laundry room across the hall from the kitchen. The design of each room was one of the reasons she loved the old place so much. The first Mr.

Marin, Ms. Marta's great-grandpa, who built the hacienda, had carefully considered every detail for comfort
and convenience. Today the laundry room boasted three
washing machines and dryers that had been added in
one of the more recent renovations that had occurred
over the years, a long narrow table for folding towels,
a hanging rack, a fold-down ironing board attached to
the wall and a deep laundry sink. A chute from an upstairs hall closet allowed the clothes to fall into a bin,
and a dumbwaiter carried the clean clothes back up.
The room was as large as the kitchen and two window
seats offered a cool, comfortable place to rest. For the
past couple of years, Adele had curled up on one and
studied for tests while she did the laundry.

Even with the age of the hacienda and the bits of rust
on the lids of the machines the place still held a charm
lacking in so many other homes. And this was just the
laundry room. All seventeen rooms were the same with
ornate moldings and baseboards, huge walk-in closets
with double panel doors, and raised ceilings. There was
even a grand staircase that as kids she and Raoul slid
down, receiving constant threats of discipline if they
were caught again.

The rooms were large and airy with arched windows
and lots of places to hide. It had been the perfect place
to grow up, but even as a child she could see things that
needed to be repaired. It just hadn't mattered because
life was good and she felt safe, loved and happy.

But the question that had occupied her mind since
Raoul's shocking statement was whether she had a right
to fight for this lovely old hacienda. To keep it in the

family—of which she was not a member. Raoul's words rang in her head: *I can't stick to one course because I have to always consider what will happen to you.* How naive had she been?

Hanging the last of her dad's shirts she returned to the kitchen to finish preparations for tomorrow's meal. The newlywed Fuentes wives had taken a lot of the work off her this year. Usually she had it all to do unless Raoul's mother was there. But Marta spent six months of the year in the beautiful mountains of North Carolina until cold weather set in. She returned to the hacienda during the winter months and left as soon as hot weather hit the valley.

Adele sliced the potatoes and put them on to cook. She'd let them cool overnight and mix the ingredients for potato salad in the morning. She put the tea on to brew and laid out a huge bag of rice, garlic and *tomate*. Carina and Kayla were making the salad and desserts and the men already had the smoker going, cooking the brisket and *barbacoa*.

The house was silent and dark since she'd been in the kitchen and laundry room all evening and hadn't taken the time to turn on the lights. Her dad retired to his room shortly after supper and she'd been left alone with her thoughts. Raoul had flown to Alaska the day after returning from Padre Island. The new customers had asked him to visit their warehouse. They needed help making the place conducive to preserving grapefruits until they could be placed in stores. Normally he called her with questions or simply shared the highlights of his trip but the phone had not rung all week long.

Most often during those conversations she ranted and raved at him because he spent money they didn't have.

She rinsed the soaked pinto beans and placed even amounts into four different Crock-Pots, to let them cook through the night. Her charro beans were a favorite amongst the workers and they declared them the best in the whole Rio Grande Valley. She wondered if the Fuentes brothers still remembered the burnt smell from her first few attempts to cook them at age fourteen. You sure couldn't go off and swim in the arroyo for a couple of hours while the beans were on high heat. Had her dad not rescued the smoldering pot it would have burned the house to the ground. That would have solved their problem for sure.

She wiped off the countertops, emptied the dishwasher and with nothing left to occupy her hands went to sit on the window seat, waiting for the last load of laundry to finish. With a shiver of vivid recollection, she examined Raoul's words again. In all the years she'd lived at the hacienda, she'd never been made to feel like an outsider. It was her home; her family. She'd received the same punishment as the boys, been rewarded when they were rewarded. Marta Fuentes had mothered her, had taken her to piano lessons and recitals. To go anywhere, do anything, she'd asked permission, same as the boys. It was just like being family—except that she called her Ms. Marta instead of mom.

But make no mistake, as the owner of the hacienda I will make the final decision. Raoul definitely was the owner. She'd been there when they read the last will and testament of Ms. Marta's dad. Each grandson retained shares in the property but Raoul held the most. So where did that leave her? The thought tore at her insides.

Momentary panic gnawed away at her confidence. The tension had increased dramatically this past year between herself and Raoul; everyone who knew them could vouch for that. She took a deep breath and tried to relax. It didn't work. She put both hands in her hair and all but screamed. Why, why, why was this happening? She climbed off the window seat and began to pace. She floundered. She felt set adrift. Dismayed at the feelings in her gut, she briefly thought about praying, but her prayers most often went unanswered.

She sensed his presence before she ever saw him. It had always been like that. She looked up and sure enough Raoul leaned casually against the door frame. He studied her with his enigmatic gaze, his eyes sharp and assessing. Disconcerted, she crossed her arms and looked away. She didn't know this Raoul. And she had no clue what to say to him or where she stood.

He walked forward, stopping in front of her. She waited in silence. It annoyed her no end that her hands were shaking. In their childhood she would have fought him tooth and nail if he threatened her, but it had been quite a few years since she'd held him down until he cried uncle. The grown man in front of her now towered over her.

"I owe you an apology."

Her mind refused to register the significance of his words. She stared at him, baffled. "What did you say?" She could hardly lift her voice above a whisper.

"I should never have treated you like that." He looked

at his hands and seemed almost hesitant to speak. She bit down hard on her lower lip. She wanted to scream at him. Unload all the fears and frustrations he'd caused her this past week. Uncertainty kept her quiet.

"You belong here at The Queen as much as I do. This is your home and there will always be a place for you here, even if we lose her."

She opened her mouth to protest but his jaw visibly tensed and his mouth firmed.

"Let me finish, Della." He held up a hand to silence her. "I will do everything humanly possible to bring financial stability to my inheritance, exactly as my brothers have done with theirs. But if we can't pull The Queen out of the downward spiral she's been in the last ten years, then we will cut our losses and downsize or we'll lose everything."

He turned on his heel and strode to the door. He stood there a moment, his back to her. "And, Della." She met his gaze full on when he turned back to her. "I am no longer the little asthmatic boy you cared for and bullied to make stronger. I outgrew that sickness before my twelfth birthday. And while I will always appreciate your loyalty and care during that time, I cannot allow the disrespect and nagging to continue. As of right now, that stops. *Comprende?*"

She stared wordlessly across at him, her heart pounding. Through the roaring din, she breathed one word. *"Comprende."* Yes, she understood perfectly. There had just been a shift in power at the Citrus Queen.

Raoul stretched out on the bed, weariness in every bone of his body. Why had no one warned him that stress could tire a man much more than a hard day's work? All week long, he'd been plagued by uneasiness. Della had changed. He didn't know this new person. She'd gone on vacation without telling him. He hadn't known whether she'd be here or not when he got back today, and the indecision about whether to call or not had chewed up his insides.

He found no difficulty telling his brothers to get over it or get therapy; why oh why did he find it so hard to do the same with Adele? Everybody has issues, so why did she think she had the monopoly on problems? Better yet, how could he help her get over hers? Life's many curves and bumps could be looked upon as a challenge. But Adele was filled with fear. He found it hard to accept that idea. She had bullied him through childhood, challenging him to climb trees, swim and run a bit farther when his lungs threatened to burst. She had never been afraid of anything. How did he reconcile the girl of his youth to the woman of today?

That same girl had slept on the floor by his bed on the nights asthma tightened his chest and made it hard to breathe. She would climb in the dumbwaiter and go downstairs for cold water when he was thirsty, braving the monsters that hid in the shadows of their imagination. She beat up the school bully for mocking his inhaler use, and she even put on a frilly dress she hated and went to the prom with him when his date dumped him at the last minute.

Suspended somewhere between exhaustion and sleep, his last thoughts were of the Scripture the new pastor had taken his message from the previous Sunday.

The psalmist had written about how pleasant it was to live in peace with those around you. Raoul prayed it would come true with him and Della. He wasn't sure how much longer he could take the strain.

Adele raced down the stairs, her flip-flops slapping against the gleaming oak wood. How could she have overslept? She took the cooled potatoes from the fridge and began to add the ingredients for potato salad. Her dad carried in a huge stainless-steel pan of brisket and covered it with foil.

"Morning, Adele." He gave her name the Spanish pronunciation making the *d* a *th* sound so that her name sounded like Uh-thel-uh. For the better part of her life she had simply felt American. But one never forgot their Spanish heritage around her dad. He wore the white shirts with front pleats, khaki pants and the cowboy-looking hat known as a sombrero. He spoke Tex-Mex, meaning he'd start a sentence in one language and finish it with the easiest words in the other.

She'd never known him to be very emotional, not since the day Marta Fuentes and her husband had all but carried him from his wife's graveside. Great heaving sobs had shaken his body and Adele had stumbled along behind them uncertain whether she should follow or not, unsure about where she fit in. Pretty much like she'd felt for the past month—and the major reason she couldn't fall asleep last night.

"Popi, why didn't you wake me? Now I'm running behind." She glanced at the clock on the microwave over the stove. "They will be here at noon, so I only have two hours to get it all together." She could hear the whine in her voice and Raoul's words whipped through her mind. This, too, had to stop. "Sorry, Popi. I will get it done."

Her dad paused midstep. He appeared bewildered by her apology.

"What?" She felt like screaming in frustration. "I can't apologize to my own dad?"

"Apology accepted." He shrugged and continued to the sink. Swiping a paper towel to dry his hands he delivered his usual solemn comments. "I just don't remember it ever happening before."

Irked by his cool, aloof manner, she pretended to look for something in the refrigerator when he started to say something else. All of a sudden it seemed as if no one liked her for who she was. She felt as if she'd been tried and had come up lacking big-time. Her confidence had taken some direct hits she wasn't sure she'd recover from anytime soon.

She cleaned the kitchen, then filled cups with ice and set them back in the freezer. In the walk-in pantry she gathered paper plates, plastic utensils and napkins and set them on the island, ready for use. She hauled the commercial coffeemaker from the pantry and filled it with water and grounds, the coffee's aroma making her stomach growl. If only coffee tasted as good as it smelled.

Mentally checking off the list of things she had to do, she started upstairs for a quick shower when she heard Raoul call her name. She wavered between ignoring him or answering. After last night she figured she ought to behave in the desired manner.

"In here." She started back down the stairs and headed to the kitchen. Raoul had set several bags on the island top, so she started unloading. Ten loaves of light bread. Later she threw the store bags in the trash.

"I bought canned soft drinks to put in the coolers so we don't have cups to deal with. They should be cold by lunchtime."

With both hands on her hips she confronted him. "You…" She struggled to hide her annoyance. Why hadn't he asked her first? Surely he remembered that everyone loved her tea. She gritted her teeth to keep from railing at him. All that time she'd wasted filling the ice cups, much less making bucket loads of tea. So she was expected to let things like this pass? And play nice? She could do that, but it went against the grain. Trying to sound nonchalant, her voice raised an octave. "You did?"

"I thought it would save you from having to make tea and ice cups. It will also help with cleanup." He stepped into the pantry and she heard him start to drag the coolers from under the bottom shelves. She helped him fill both coolers with bagged ice and the drinks. They finished and he threw the ice bags in the trash then dried his hands with a paper towel. "Okay, what else do you need help with?"

Adele hesitated, blinking with bafflement. Welcoming the confusion, she took a moment to think before speaking. Really! First an ultimatum, then an apology, and now the offer of help. "I think we've covered everything." She pointed to the area on the island countertop beside the waiting paper plates and utensils. "The food will go there and we'll form a buffet line down both sides, same as always." The routine was the same but nothing in her life seemed familiar.

"I'm impressed with how you carry this off every year." He leaned against the sink and crossed his arms. Keenly aware of his scrutiny, she chose her words carefully.

"I love doing it. Everyone has a great time and we celebrate our independence. It's a great feeling, you know. Not being under anyone's authority but your own... Having the freedom of choice but obeying because we love and cherish something we've worked so hard for."

She looked up into eyes dark and probing. He stared at her speculatively. To her utter disbelief and further humiliation, she dropped her head and walked away. What in the world was wrong with her?

Chapter 5

"Knock, knock?"

Adele looked out her bathroom door and called loudly, "It's open. Come on in."

Carina poked her head around the bedroom door and laughed as she spoke. "Are you decent?"

"Yes. I'm almost ready." She gave her hair a last toweled squeeze, then turned back to the mirror to fluff her curls, the bane of her existence.

"You're late, girly." Kayla followed behind Carina, teasing laughter in her voice. "The most perfect Adele not on time. The world is coming to an end." She sat down on the freshly made bed, unaware that Adele's lips puckered with annoyance. There were three chairs in her room so why couldn't Kayla sit in one? Now there'd be puffy places Adele would have to smooth out before she followed them downstairs. Her eyes met Carina's in the mirror. Carina shrugged, her look mingled with both rebuke and sympathy. Shame filled Adele for being aggravated at something so trivial as a messy comforter.

"Who's the handsome guy with Raoul?" Kayla had gone to the window and stared down into the backyard. Adele fought her compulsion to smooth the bed as she joined them. Her gaze swept over the lawn she worked so hard to keep green.

"That's the new veterinarian, Daniel Jacobs." Adele's heart leaped a tiny bit.

"You've met him already?" Excitedly Kayla continued, "Marcelo called him last night about inspecting our cattle. He seemed very nice."

"So that's the twin."

"What?" Kayla and Adele spoke simultaneously.

"The new pastor, David Jacobs—Daniel is his twin." Carina let the curtain fall back into place.

"You mean there are two new good-looking single men in the area?" Kayla's smile broadened in approval. She waggled her eyebrows at Adele.

Adele's sense of humor took over and she laughed. "I wouldn't stand a chance. Every mother in church, if they don't already, will have the pastor's calendar filled with dinner dates and home cooking. He will be married before the year's out."

"Well, there's always the brother, and from what I just saw, he's every bit as handsome as his twin," Carina said.

They stared at Carina and then all three burst out laughing.

"Ya think?" Kayla snorted.

"They're twins, Carina." Adele knew Carina's wide-eyed innocence was merely a smoke screen. She was one of the wisest women Adele knew, humble and graceful, yet she could deliver a zing with the best of them.

They started down the stairs single file, all three resting their hands on the wide banister. Adele came last. It would be the only time this evening she was as tall as her friends. A whistle shrilled through the air as the Fuentes brothers entered the foyer. Adele smiled as the men admired their wives, Kayla teasing Marcelo that he didn't know the difference between flip-flops and high heels. Then Adele looked into eyes black as coal as Raoul paused in the doorway to the living room. When they neared the bottom, Juan Antonio extended his hand and escorted Carina the last two steps. Marcelo followed suit. And then it was Adele's turn. Raoul took two steps toward her but a movement to her left caught her attention and Daniel Jacobs took her hand, placing it in the crook of his arm.

"Hello, beautiful." The warmth of his smile echoed in his voice. Adele's lips parted in surprise. She glanced quickly at Raoul. There was an arrested expression on his face, then his eyebrow raised a fraction and he turned and followed the others.

Adele looked a long way up to find Daniel staring down at her. She didn't miss his obvious examination and approval. Was he interested in her? Her pulse quickened at the speculation.

"Adele." Alma Cantu called her name and gave her a

hug, effectively removing her from Daniel's arm. Alma worked for Kayla at Confetti and had become one of Adele's close friends. She positioned Adele so no one could see her, then mouthed, "Who's the good-looking guy?"

Had Adele not been conscious of Daniel's close scrutiny, she'd have laughed out loud at Alma's curiosity. Instead, she turned and introduced them, slipping away while they got to know each other.

She helped the orchard workers' wives carry food to the kitchen. The noise level increased and a person had to be in the depths of despair not to get swept up into the happiness of the occasion. Adele felt her spirits soar. There was nothing like a good day with family and friends celebrating the great United States of America's independence.

The new pastor prayed before the meal, his voice resonant and impressive as he remembered the battles the nation had faced in the past and were facing now, and how gracious God was to give victory to such undeserving people. Adele felt movement beside her and peeked to see Alma snatch a tissue from the table behind them. Her own eyes had filled with tears of gratitude. She slid her arm around Alma's waist and they stood together, their hearts in one accord. What a wonderful prayer. What a great nation. What a powerful God.

When the prayer ended everyone called in unison a loud Amen and Raoul set off the first round of firecrackers. It startled everyone but seemed to set the mood for the rest of the evening.

There was enough food to feed everyone and Adele

sent leftovers home with anyone who wanted them. By five o'clock everyone had gone, the house had been straightened up and the men had finished cleaning the outside. Adele, Carina and Kayla sank tiredly into the cushiony seating in the family *sala,* it being the smaller sitting room, more personal and comfortable. The other girls chose recliners, sighing as they put their feet up, and Adele stretched her legs out on the sofa, her mood still buoyant.

"What a great day, but boy am I pooped. I can only imagine how you feel, Adele, with all the cleaning and preparations you did to make this such a huge success." Carina yawned, her lids closing sleepily over her eyes.

"I agree. And you do it every year," Kayla added.

"But everyone pitches in and helps. Even Raoul did this year." Adele had always thought the effort worthwhile. "By the way, the desserts were wonderful. I kept three pieces of the chess bar cake and enough banana pudding for Daddy and Raoul."

"I can't believe those chess bars turned out so well. I made three pans and I just knew one of them would fall flat but thank the Lord it didn't." Kayla owned Confetti, a party store that catered as a sideline. She was forevermore trying new recipes and the family members were recipients of such good fortune. Marcelo claimed it added to his waistline but the evidence didn't support his claim.

Carina stood and stretched, then suggested they go for a walk. "If I go to sleep, I won't feel like riding to the island to watch the fireworks, so let's get moving." They started a fast-paced stroll down the mile-long driveway.

"How did Raoul help?" Carina huffed between breaths.

"Help with what?" Adele turned to ask Carina and found herself studied with curious intensity. "Oh, with preparations," she said, remembering her previous statement. She explained about the canned drinks and ice. "It's so frustrating." At Kayla's incredulous look she hurried on. "I mean, really! Can he not just ask what's needed instead of doing his own thing? Is that too much to ask?"

There was an awkward silence and Adele looked inquiringly at her friends. "What?"

"You know, Adele—" Kayla's tone of voice definitely lacked sympathy with Adele's plight "—compromise won't kill you. You could try meeting Raoul halfway."

"How do you mean?"

"Well, you plan this celebration every year, right?"

"Yes."

"Then why don't you make a list and share it with Raoul and your dad and then everyone will know what's expected of them." Kayla's mind worked exactly as her business major had taught her. "You did it with us on the desserts and that worked out well and…" She paused as if carefully choosing her next words.

"What?"

"I feel strongly that I should say this but I don't want to hurt your feelings." Even though Kayla had married the oldest Fuentes brother, she lacked the maturity and sensitivity of Carina.

"Just say it, Kayla."

"Well, there have been times when I thought you should have cut Raoul some slack."

Startled hurt turned into anger. Adele forced her lips to part in a curved, stiff smile. "Really," she retorted in cold sarcasm.

"Now don't get angry with me. I'm only trying to help. I don't like to see you so burdened down with all the things you have to do for The Queen, but Raoul works, too. He…"

Adele interrupted in a rush of words. "Works at what, exactly?" She took a deep breath and tried to relax the rigidity in her shoulders. She watched Kayla swallow hard and her hand shook as she pushed her hair behind her ear, but she lifted her chin and boldly met Adele's gaze.

"Do you actually think The Queen would still be running without his help, Adele? Are you really that naive?" Kayla's face flushed and Adele knew it wasn't from the walk. She felt a shock run through her. Kayla was one of her dearest friends. But she sure seemed upset with Adele.

"I'm not sure what you're getting at."

"Well, I could be mistaken, but someone keeps the orchards running smoothly. And doesn't he contract the buyers? I know your dad does a lot of the book work, but someone has to give the workers instructions and oversee production. And from what I understand, you don't have a foreman, so…" Kayla shrugged and then continued in a gentler tone of voice. "It just stands to reason that he does quite a bit of the work to keep this place going and I know that Marcelo speaks highly of him and seems very confident that he's handling the job correctly."

They had stopped walking and stood looking at each other. Adele glanced at Carina for support, but Carina's gaze dropped to her shoes. So, Carina felt the same as Kayla. Adele searched anxiously for the meaning behind Kayla's hurtful words but came up with nothing. A quick and disturbing thought penetrated the blankness of her mind and with it came clarity.

She felt the dull ache of foreboding. Assailed by a terrible sense of bitterness, she spoke with as reasonable a voice as she could manage. "I'll think about what you've said, Kayla. Maybe I need to look at things from another person's perspective." First and foremost in Adele's mind was restoring the relationship with her friends. She didn't want to lose them over a sorry, lazy man. But apparently she was meant to carry her burdens alone. Complaining to others would get her nowhere.

"You know, Adele," Carina's voice soothed, "you could talk to Pastor Jacobs about the load you carry. Maybe he could give you spiritual counsel that would encourage you and point you in the right direction with the feelings you have. Sometimes we can turn things around with something as simple as a positive attitude. It might help."

"Sure. I'll do that." *When donkeys fly,* Adele thought.

They moved to the side of the road when they heard a vehicle approaching from the hacienda. Marcelo pulled even with them, and Juan Antonio and Daniel Jacobs climbed down from the cab of the truck. Marcelo called Kayla's name.

"You wanna go with me to feed? Won't take me long and we'll come right back." It was plain as the nose on his face that he was head over heels in love with the beautiful Kayla and couldn't bear to be away from her any length of time. The fast way she climbed into the truck proved she felt the same.

Juan Antonio wrapped an arm around Carina's shoulders and teased. "I wasn't sure you knew the way back. Thought you might need a knight in shining armor."

Carina leaned up on tiptoe for a kiss and murmured something that made him chuckle, and then they started back to the hacienda, leaving Adele and Daniel to follow.

"That's what love should look like."

Startled from her thoughts at Daniel's words, Adele stared at the couple walking in front of them. Juan Antonio and Carina had fought all odds to be together and it had paid off. One just had to listen to their conversation a few moments to recognize respect, honor and pure adoration.

"You're so right."

"Thanks for the meal and the entertainment. I had a fantastic time." He slowed his steps to match her shorter stride.

"I'm glad you came and it was good to meet your brother. He's very impressive. I loved his prayer and he seems the perfect pastor material for our church. I can't wait to hear him preach."

"I haven't seen you in any of the services. I wasn't sure you attended there."

"Been attending there since I was seven, but the last

couple of weeks I haven't gotten to go. I had graduation and then took a week of vacation." A tiny nagging voice accused Adele and rightly so. She could have gone this past Sunday, but her mind had been in such turmoil she had stayed in bed and wallowed over her misfortunes. "Life sometimes gangs up on me." She laughed self-consciously. "Or so it seems."

"I know exactly what you mean. My week has been like that."

Adele looked closely at him. He stared at the road in front of him, head down, a frown furrowing his brow. "You want to talk about it?"

"I'll have to talk to your dad or Raoul sooner or later. The state says my office must have at least one acre with a corral so I can house sick livestock. There's acreage behind the office I'm renting from you now, but it has no corral and it has to be coded as livestock approved. That won't happen where I'm at so I have till August to find a new place."

"Oh, my, that is a problem." Adele gave in to the tension that had been building all day, her mind swirling with frustration and panic. *Now we will lose this renter, and there goes the extra money. We take one step forward and three steps backward.* "Just when we were getting used to the extra money." She struggled to keep her comment lighthearted.

"I know." He shrugged. "I love the location. It's central to both counties." Adele could sense his disappointment. "I will have to look for another place and I just got settled in. Such an aggravation." He shook his head regretfully. Then he transferred his gaze to her and a strange, faintly eager look flashed in his eyes. "But I don't intend my problems to ruin this fantastic day. Tell me about this trip to the island. What can I expect?"

"Noise. Lots of noise and beautiful lights. The fireworks are breathtaking. The best I have ever seen."

"Will it be crowded?"

"Oh, yeah." Adele's mood seemed suddenly buoyant. It felt good to have someone interested in what she had to say. "But we have a winter Texan friend from Michigan with a house there. We have the keys and we check the place out from time to time for him. It's right on the bay so we have a front row seat. It takes forever after the fireworks end to get off the island. The cars are bumper to bumper, so we cross over in Juan Antonio's boat."

"Sounds like fun."

"Oh, it is. We grill hamburgers on the deck and wait for darkness to fall. It's great. One of my favorite times of the year. No stress or worries bother me when I see those designs and colors light up the sky. All appears well with God and the world."

Daniel chuckled. "What could possibly worry someone as young as you?"

"Hah." The word spewed from her mouth. "Do you have till the middle of next week? 'Cause it would take that long to unload all my worries on you." She plunged on carelessly, Kayla's put-down fresh in her mind. "The biggest being the loss of the hacienda."

"The hacienda is in jeopardy?"

Adele looked at him in disbelief. Who talked like that? *Jeopardy?* But then he was a gringo and white people always surprised her. "Well, in the words of Raoul, it's a money pit. Seems like the upkeep drains us every time we get our heads above water."

The grand house came into view, and even in disrepair it almost took one's breath away.

"She is a beauty for sure." Daniel stopped walking and stood staring, his eyes sweeping the barely green lawn, the circular drive lined with palm trees of different sizes, the bark scattered around the place, the peeling paint on the stucco and the broken red tiles on the roof. Adele watched him and felt that while he appreciated the estate, he wasn't overly impressed. For some reason that irked her. Could he not see the history, the love and potential of restoration? His next words surprised her.

"You should contact the historical society. I imagine they'd love to get their hands on a place like this."

"You mean sell to them?" Adele could not help the hardness that entered her voice. All she needed today was another person telling her it was okay to lose her home.

"Not necessarily." He began walking again, so she kept pace beside him. She couldn't help but notice that the dead limbs needed to be trimmed on the larger palm trees, but there was no one to do it. They couldn't afford to hire someone with a bucket truck and there was no way to climb the tree with a power saw. "If I'm not mistaken, there are circumstances where the owner retains the rights to the place. They sign a contract, though, to give tours to the public. A proper history must be written, and the society assumes all responsibility for providing correct historical facts and for restoring the place while preserving its historical value. Oh, and they maintain it with state finances for as long as it stays in the owner's hands and is available to the public."

Wheels began to turn in Adele's mind. "Can the owners continue to live in it?"

They walked up the steps to the double front doors. Ten-foot doors that Adele could never open herself, which is why she always used the back or side doors. But Daniel had no such problem. They crossed the threshold and stepped into the cool interior. "I don't know. My sister dealt with them when we gave up the family home in Charleston. We had all moved out, so it was never an issue with us. Why don't you give them a call?"

Hope took wings in Adele's heart. Maybe just maybe there was a way to save the old place. She would do whatever she could to keep Raoul from leveling it to the ground.

Later that night she stared out the minibus windows, her thoughts on the events of the day. The fireworks had been worth the hour drive and the boat ride, and the camaraderie, priceless. She, Kayla and Carina had apparently buried the hatchet, laughing and teasing as if the earlier incident had never occurred, but time had brought clarity to Adele's tired mind. One fact had been driven home in her heart and it brought with it an agonizing truth: her best friends were now part of the Fuentes family. Adele was not. They were circling the wagons and Adele was the outsider.

Chapter 6

Adele pored over the Excel spreadsheets she'd printed off from her dad's computer. He had meticulously recorded every transaction for the past twenty years. She had the past three years in her hand and for every customer they'd lost, they had gained one back. But this didn't make sense. "Why aren't we financially stable?"

"Welcome to my life."

She drew a sharp breath. "Raoul." She placed a hand on her heart. "You scared the life out of me."

"Sorry. I thought you heard me come in." He sank into the chair across the desk and raked a hand through his hair. "So you're in charge now? Where'd your dad go?"

"He left with his fishing pole and tackle box. He said not to expect him back till I saw the whites of his eyes." Seeing the answering amusement in his eyes, she laughed.

He peered around the room. "You gonna change this place? Spruce it up some? It's looked like this since we were kids."

"Um, Raoul, that's something I'd like to talk to you about." Nervously she fingered a loose curl near her cheek.

"Wow! Now that's something I haven't seen in a long time," he said with a significant lift of his brows. His dark eyes were gentle and contemplative, yet she dropped the curl like a hot potato when she saw that's what had his attention. "If memory serves me right, you're either fixing to talk me into something that will get me in trouble, or you're in trouble and need help getting out." Leaning forward in his chair, he asked, "So which is it?"

She shot him a withering glance, exasperated that he'd seen right through her. "Neither. I'm taking into account our conversations from the past month and trying to do the right thing."

"And that would be?"

"Asking before I take action."

His dark eyes narrowed speculatively. "So you don't really need or want my advice, you're just following house rules."

She was too surprised to do more than stare. Did she hear disappointment in his voice? She shook her head, effectively dislodging such foolish thoughts.

"I think, from our past conversations, that I may need your permission." She opened the desk drawer and removed a folder. "And even if I didn't, I'd want your input." She opened the folder and turned it toward him. He slid to the edge of his chair and pulled the papers from within.

"What am I looking at here?"

"It's a proposal for what I'd like to do with this office." The building her dad had used when he wasn't working in the hacienda had two rooms plus a bath and a tacked on mudroom/washroom. A walk-in closet had been turned into a file-slash-junk room. Its location was perfect for her plans because it could be accessed without passing through the electronic gates that protected the private drive to the hacienda. It in fact was attached to the gatehouse which hadn't been used even once in Adele's lifetime. The wall that ran the property line was an extension of the front of the office. There was a tall arch over the road with the famous design of the Alamo that connected an exact replica of her dad's office but no one had used that side in years. The bell in the center at the top of the arch had rusted and looked a little lopsided but the ambience of the place never failed to move her.

She waited quietly while he read the terms of the rental agreement she'd drawn up, and then he looked at her, confusion evident in the first words he spoke. "Why would Daniel want to rent this place? He just signed the contract on the frontage office on the main highway."

She explained the circumstances. "So we could rent this place to him. He'd have room out back to house injured animals, and with his rent and a possible new renter on the frontage road, we'd have better cash flow."

"And where would you put this office?"

"In the sewing room at the hacienda." Concerned about his answer, she rushed on. "It's never used for anything other than storage. I never sew and your mother doesn't, either, anymore when she's here. It's big enough for the equipment we have in here and then some. Plus it opens onto the veranda by the drive so potential customers would never enter the house."

"What does Daniel say about this?"

"I haven't asked him yet. I wanted to run it by you first."

He seemed lost in thought for a bit, and then he grinned at her. "You know what, Della?" The warmth of his smile echoed in his voice. "This is the second financial breakthrough in less than a month. First the new Alaskan customers, now this. If we keep it up, who knows what might happen."

She felt strangely flattered by his words and a ripple of excitement rushed through her. They'd had a conversation and made a decision together, without arguing. She leaned back in her chair, relaxing and soaking up the feeling of contentment. "My first day on the job and I'm happy, I've made you happy and I'm certain Daniel will be happy."

Raoul's expression stilled and grew serious. "Is that important to you?"

"Yes." She shook her head decisively. "I would love to turn our financial situation around."

He raised a hand dismissively. "I meant Daniel. Is it important to you that he's happy?"

To her annoyance she found herself starting to

blush. She shrugged to hide her confusion. "I guess," she stammered. "After all, he is our renter so his happiness counts a lot."

There were touches of humor around his dark eyes and his firm mouth curled as if always on the edge of laughter.

"You sat together on the trip to the island to see the fireworks and then he didn't leave your side till we got back home." His fingers, tapered and strong, rubbed the arm of his chair and he shifted around, pulling his ankle up to rest across the other knee. If she didn't know better she would think he was nervous. "I just wondered if there was something going on between the two of you."

"He's a good friend. I like talking to him and as you can see, it could be beneficial to us."

"Hmm." He stood and turned to leave, so Adele couldn't see his expression, but the seriousness of the moment made her think he was a bit upset about her involvement with Daniel. Such as it was.

"Where are you going?" Not that it was any of her business since he was the boss, but old habits die hard and he seemed to forget that fact as often as she did.

"The picker lift broke down out in orchard six. I thought I'd go see what I can do to get it running again." His voice sounded weary and Adele studied him, trying to see things in the light of what Kayla had said. She watched him rotate his shoulders in an effort to relieve tension or pain. He tilted his head to first one side then the other.

"Do you have a headache?"

"Splitting."

She went around the desk toward him. "Sit down and I'll fix it." He'd had headaches since she'd known him and sometimes they put him in bed for a day or two. She motioned him to a wooden chair. "Put your arms across the back and lay your head on them."

He protested. "Della, I took two Excedrin tablets barely an hour ago. It hasn't had time to kick in."

The outer door opened and Marcelo walked in. "What's up, compadres?"

Adele answered before Raoul had a chance. "He has a headache and took medicine an hour ago and it hasn't worked yet. You know what that means." She pointed to the chair again.

"Della, for years now, I've managed without your massages. I think I can handle this one."

"Something is seriously wrong with you, bro." Marcelo sat in the chair Adele had just vacated and repositioned the computer screen to his liking. "Never turn down a massage." He began to search for something and Raoul, realizing Adele had no intention of relenting, blew an exasperated breath and did as she asked.

Adele started at the crown of his head, gently touching each pressure point. When she reached his neck and shoulders, she kneaded the muscles, finding each sore spot, squeezing and massaging until the knots disappeared and his shoulders were loose and flexible. She'd watched his mother circumvent many sick days for him by doing this very thing and in high school she'd stepped in when Ms. Marta's hands became tired.

In less than fifteen minutes he was sound asleep and she tiptoed round to where Marcelo worked. They both knew the sleep would help Raoul more than anything, so they carried on a whispered conversation and Adele helped him find the information he needed. Then she shared the rental proposal with him. She felt a glow of achievement at his praise of her idea.

He patted her on top of the head as he left. "Thanks, short stuff." She rolled her eyes at him, but smiled. He was her favorite and he knew it. "I'll be back later today to sign that rental agreement with Daniel Jacobs if he agrees to it."

She nodded at him and he left quietly, easing the door shut. Each brother held a percentage in the rental properties they owned and her dad had finalized the legalities stating that each brother must sign, else the contract wasn't valid. He concluded it would keep things aboveboard and prevent takeovers or arguments.

So far, two brothers liked her idea, and she felt certain Juan Antonio would, too. And there was no doubt Daniel would. She picked up her keys and the proposal and started to the door.

"Where you going?" Raoul sat up, rubbing the sleep from his eyes, his voice husky and low. At times like this she felt such affection for him. Her gaze fell to the strong jawline, then his humorous, kind mouth. Her feelings for him were so tangled up, confusing to the point of despair. Like daisy petals, she loved him, she loved him not. At one point she had fancied herself *in love* with him. But aggravation and exasperation and finally futility convinced her that to love him would be emotional suicide.

She raised her eyes to find him watching her, a contemplative yet curious expression on his handsome face. A subtle hint of something stirred between them. She felt it and she knew by his waiting silence that he did, too. She took a quick breath of utter astonishment. He was her friend, nothing more. To care for him in any other way would be and had been detrimental to her sanity. She blinked. Holding the proposal up, she enlightened him. "I thought I'd see if Daniel agrees to this."

He walked to her and took the folder. "I'll do that." He pulled one of her curls straight, then watched it bounce back into place. He'd done that often when they were kids, but it had never caused butterflies in the pit of her stomach. And he'd never looked at her like this before.

The office door slammed behind him. She stood motionless in the middle of the room, her thoughts and emotions in utter chaos.

As Daniel signed the rental agreement Della had drawn up, Raoul studied the man. He guessed Daniel was okay to look at; he didn't have any facial deformities, no scars and his ears were about even on each side of his head. He stood about an inch taller than Raoul himself, but the taller they were the harder they'd fall. So, what did Della possibly see in him?

For some reason that escaped him at the moment. It rattled his cage that Daniel and Adele had spent so much time together on the island. He'd heard Adele's laughter, seen her eyes light up; she'd even placed her hand on Daniel's arm while she explained something. And

Daniel...well, one thing Raoul knew was a man on the prowl. He couldn't take his eyes off her. And he hadn't said three words to the other ladies in the group. That made Raoul's stomach sour and he rubbed it absently.

"Now, that's what I call a sweet deal."

Raoul accepted the contract and shook Daniel's extended hand. "Glad you're happy." He put the papers back in the folder. "I'll let you know when it's ready for you to move in." He turned to leave and a thought turned him back. "Will this bring a lot of traffic to our place?"

"It shouldn't. I'll be the one transporting the animals back and forth."

"Do you use chemicals or anything that will harm the fruit trees? Anything that will seep into the ground?"

Daniel looked at him as if he had two heads. "Man, do you not read your own contracts?"

The man's attitude could use an adjustment and Raoul thought he might be able to help him in that area. "What do you mean?"

"It's there in black and white. The contract states there can be no chemicals—not even feed, garbage or refuse—brought onto the property that might cause damage."

"Oh." Raoul felt a little foolish. "Della thinks of everything." *Especially,* he thought, *if it threatens her precious Queen in any way.*

"That's why I'm glad she'll be working for me."

Momentarily speechless in surprise, Raoul stared at the man in disbelief. "I'm sorry. What did you say?"

With long purposeful strides, Daniel walked to the

filing cabinet and placed his copy of the contract inside. Then he faced Raoul, the beginning of a smile tipping the corners of his mouth. "Before she graduated, she agreed to work twenty or so hours a week for me."

Raoul needed to get out of the office before he did or said something and ruined the contract the ink wasn't even dry on. Plus, he could not hear over the roaring in his ears. So much for Della's claim that she needed to talk things over with him. He should have known. She'd never before asked anyone for help or direction. How foolish he'd been to think she had changed. He managed a sensible goodbye, then climbed into his car, anger and panic vying for equal attention.

How long had Adele and Daniel known each other? He thought they'd just met at the Fourth of July meal. And why would she agree to work for someone else when she barely had time to take care of him and her dad?

He raced up the drive, his truck eating the mile-long road in less than half the time it normally took. Her words from this morning were purely a sham. She had no plans to run decisions by him; like always she did what she wanted. His anger and hurt knew no limits.

Oh, great. His brothers' trucks were parked outside. Just what he needed. Happiness oozed from the two. He entered the office, a man on a mission. Marcelo sat with his feet on the desk and Juan Antonio paced back and forth on the other side.

"What took you so long? Adele called over an hour ago and said you'd gone to show the proposal to Daniel and would have the signed contract back in a few min-

utes. She already took one load of files to the house."
Normally the most patient one in the bunch, Juan Antonio's voice held pure exasperation.

His attitude and Della's betrayal unleashed the pent-up anger in Raoul that had simmered for months. Both brothers had received one sweet deal of an inheritance but he'd been given a run-down monstrosity with employees past retirement age and no place to go. He worked his tail off every day and it still didn't make a dent in what was needed. He tossed the folder on the desk. His voice heavy with sarcasm, he mocked, "What's the matter, J.T.? Afraid the little wifey-poo might be upset if you're late getting home?"

Juan Antonio took an abrupt step toward him, his dark eyes boring into Raoul. Raoul stiffened in defense, but Juan Antonio opened the folder and signed his name to the contract, vexation evident in every move. He brushed by Raoul and the door slammed behind him.

Marcelo had lowered his feet at Raoul's comment and now he stared curiously at him. "That went well." His caustic tone had the desired effect and Raoul felt a sense of shame at his behavior. The last of his resentment faded and he sank into the chair opposite Marcelo.

"Want to talk about it?"

"Not really."

"Good. The last thing I need today is to play nanny to a spoiled brat." Amusement flickered in the eyes that met his but Raoul also saw caring and acceptance, which made him feel worse than a mongrel dog.

"You're not helping any, Marc."

"Well, if you'd tell me what made you all aggro, I might figure it out."

Raoul wrestled with the choice to unload on his big brother or keep it to himself. Marcelo sat still, silently observing the emotional struggle Raoul felt certain showed on his face. It was a tribute to how well Adele got under his skin. He'd learned a long time ago not to spill his guts to his brothers, hiding behind a sarcastic veneer, often goading his brothers into a fight rather than showing hurt.

"Did you know Della's going to work for Daniel Jacobs?"

"Ah." Marcelo nodded once. "I figured she had something to do with this."

"Why would you think that?"

His brother had the audacity to laugh.

"You're joking, right?" At Raoul's quizzical look, he exclaimed, "Nothing and no one ever riles you like she does."

"Why would she keep something like that a secret? Just tell me that. Better yet, pull the knife out of my back." Raoul felt his mouth drop open when Marcelo stood up, preparing to leave. "Where you going? I thought you were going to help me."

"The only person that can help you with this is Adele. I didn't know she'd gone to work for him. But I can tell you from past experience with Kayla, this could be cleared up if you'd ask the woman herself. I can just about guarantee there's a simple explanation. And one thing for certain about Adele, she's not a backstabber. She's the most honest person I know."

Chapter 7

Adele stood back and surveyed her handiwork. The sewing room made the perfect office. Large and comfortable with lots of light from the floor-to-ceiling arched windows. It had taken her the better part of two weeks to clear out old files, shred documents and record addresses on the computer, but she had narrowed the filing system down to two cabinets and one of those drawers now housed the records of Daniel Jacobs.

A conference table with eight leather chairs sat directly in front of the three tall windows. She'd found the chairs in various spots around the hacienda; they belonged to a dining set from the past. Marta Fuentes could never bear to part with anything handed down through the years, which meant the house was full of antiques; some good, some not so good. In this case,

Adele knew they added an elegance fit for the grandest office. She'd taken the covers off the sewing table and found pure oak that matched the chairs and her desk. She'd had to ask Daniel to help her move it from the library; he'd placed it on rollers and they had carefully guided it across the foyer, through the formal dining room to where it sat right now.

Plants had been added, pictures that had been stored in closets now hung on the walls and from the estate office the only thing she'd taken was the aerial map of the property.

"You ready?"

She smiled at Daniel, grabbed her purse and walked through the door he held open. They were on their way to the office supply store; she to buy a new copier and Daniel to pick up flyers for his business. Adele could have made them for him but the office copier had come over on the ark and worked only in black and white. She'd just received her first paycheck from Daniel for two weeks of work and she felt giddy with excitement. And while the amount wasn't enough to cover a major expense, it sure would go a long way to needed repairs and light remodeling. She'd found an excellent deal on a copier and Daniel was purchasing the ink. Sweet. The only annoyance that spoiled an otherwise pleasant experience was that Raoul had gone missing again. So what else was new? He might have had to actually break a sweat.

"Something wrong?"

Her mood suddenly buoyant she answered truthfully. "Not a thing."

It felt good to be out of the house. Two weeks without even a trip to the store would drive some people crazy, but she had loved every moment. She'd accomplished quite a bit. But a call from the new pastor alerted her to the fact that she had her priorities out of order and she had promised to be in her pew on Sunday.

Daniel slowed as he neared the gate and Adele gasped in surprise. A chain-link fence now bordered the side of the road and encompassed at least an acre at the back of the estate office. Raoul maneuvered a back hoe carrying palm trees, placing them in holes that were already dug. Not only would Daniel have an exceptional place for horses and cattle, but the landscaping would remain beautiful and not be an eyesore. Something Adele hadn't even thought of. The fence was not new and shiny, but it was straight and blended perfectly with the surroundings. Raoul had either removed it from another place or had had it stored in the barn. A lot of work had gone into this project.

Her thoughts scampered vaguely around. As casually as she could manage she asked, "Did you know about this?"

Daniel seemed surprised by the question but he answered calmly. "It would be hard not to since I've driven by here almost every day on my way to help you." He gave her an odd look. "You didn't know?"

She kept her expression under stern restraint. Appearing nonchalant she answered in a low, composed voice, "I thought he was somewhere else."

Daniel lowered the window and waved as they passed. Raoul looked directly at her. She could feel his dark eyes boring into her as they drove on by. So she had misjudged him. How often had she been wrong about him? Apparently her two best friends thought she was guilty.

"Did you call the historical society?"

Daniel's question rescued her from the guilt and confusion that lately had accompanied her every move. "No, but I checked their requirements online." She explained what she had learned and their discussion lasted until they pulled into the store parking lot.

On the way back, Daniel teased her about how long she'd vacillated between her original choice and a more expensive copier. "I should have sent the money with you and had you buy it. I don't do well with choices," she admitted. Being with Daniel had restored her previous good humor and the satisfaction of buying something they needed for the hacienda was a powerful feeling.

"I like your choices."

Adele laughed as she climbed down from his truck. "How can you say that? This is the first choice you've seen me make."

"Not true. You chose to work for me. You chose to be my friend and with a little persuasion you agreed to ice cream at Dairy Queen."

His mouth twitched with amusement and she laughed. "We both know I manipulated that stop. Dairy Queen ice cream is my weakness."

"I'm looking forward to learning all your weaknesses, Miss Rivas." His eyes filled with teasing laughter.

"I'll just bet you are." Raoul's voice stopped them

both in their tracks. He lifted the copier box from Daniel's arms and motioned Adele through the office door, allowing it to close behind them, effectively leaving Daniel standing on the outside.

"Really, Raoul," she snapped. "Have you lost your mind?" She hurried to open the door but Daniel was climbing into his truck. She waved at him and mouthed, "I'm sorry." His grin was irresistibly devastating. He winked at her and she closed the door, a slow, satisfied smile on her face…and looked right into the eyes of a tiger, and an angry one at that.

"Willacy County." She said the first thing that came into her mind. As kids it had been their secret saying to warn the other when they were in trouble. Most often it meant "get out of here fast and hide." It seemed to have lost its significance.

"So, Adele, why don't you explain your job description with Jacobs?"

She took a letter opener from her desk and cut the tape on the copier box. How had he learned she worked for Daniel? She'd meant to tell him but she hadn't seen him. "Much the same as this office. I'm putting his files on Excel and adding them to Dropbox so he can access them from his phone wherever and whenever he desires. He pays me a salary and I plan to use it for personal things."

"Personal things?"

Disconcerted, she crossed her arms and looked away. Her initial response was to tell him she did not have to answer to him and that it was none of his business, but the uncertainty of her new position made her proceed with caution. An action totally foreign to their relationship and one she majorly resented. "Female things." She was helpless to halt her embarrassment. "You know." Her cheeks burned. "It's been a long time since I bought new clothes…" She stammered to a stop, angry at herself for feeling uncomfortable. "And I can buy groceries and not take money out of the bank account." To her shocked horror, tears filled her eyes. The ultimate humiliation.

Raoul groaned. He was a monster. Marcelo had been right. There was a simple explanation, but one she shouldn't have had to tell him. He had done this to her. His childhood friend Adele would have slapped him down with an insult had he treated her as he just did. Gathering her into his arms, he held her snugly. He expected resistance and was surprised when none was offered. "I'm sorry, Della." Even with the heels she had on she barely came to his shoulders. He gathered a handful of curls and tilted her head back. Tears trembled on her eyelids and he wiped them away with his thumbs. She was the most beautiful woman he'd ever set eyes on. Her nose exquisitely dainty, her mouth temptingly curved. But it was her chin that he traced lightly. Iron determination motivated her and he'd only seen her cry once in all their years together.

She withdrew from his arms and moved to the right. She answered the phone, her voice soft and low. He hadn't heard it ring. How long had she done without? He felt sick to his stomach. She'd been in need and he'd been oblivious. She hung the phone up but kept her back to him.

"Della, we have to talk."

He saw her swallow hard. "I have a lot of work to do, Raoul. Can it wait?"

"Please, Della. I'll talk and you listen, okay?"

He waited for her consent, then struggled with what to say. He decided to go with his heart. "I was out of line. You're free to do as you want. You owe me no explanations." He leaned against the desk, facing her. "There's been a lot of uncertainty in our lives lately and I think it has put us both on edge. But instead of fighting *against* each other, let's fight *for* each other. Deal?"

He held out his fist and she bumped hers against it. He caught her hand before she could pull away. He turned her palm upward, noting the barely visible calluses. She would consider them battle wounds and be proud of them. He was humbled that most of them were because of him. He kissed her palm and glanced at her for signs of rejection. Every emotion showed on her face: interest, wonder, bemusement. And unless he read the signs wrong, there was also a tentative invitation in the questioning depth of her dark eyes. Hope sprouted wings. This was his Della. And she wasn't averse to exploring an adult relationship with him. He had just graduated from childhood friend to possible boyfriend. 'Bout time.

Adele's voice seemed to come from a long way off. Probably because she could hear her heart pounding in her ears. What was happening to her? "How do we fight for each other?" She had longed for this since her teens; for him to see her as something other than his best pal.

Raoul had retreated across the room and stood staring out through the window at the front lawn. "By talking things over. Planning together. Getting our ducks in a row, as your dad would say." He made a dismissive gesture and turned to face her. "I'm tired of all the fighting. Remember, Della, when we felt like we could conquer the world? We can. If we work together. Even the Bible says two are better than one. And your dad was an excellent worker, but he had no vision for this place other than keeping a roof over your head. But it's within our reach to make a success of this place." He grinned and straightened his shoulders. "What do you say?"

Excitement warmed her, melting the last of the ice that had surrounded her heart for so long. "Yes," she answered quickly, eagerly.

He gave her a quick hug. She compared the awkward hug of graduation night to the ones she'd received today. She exhaled a long sigh of contentment. Totally different. His hands slid down her arms and caught her wrists. "This feels right, doesn't it?" An expression of satisfaction showed in his beautiful eyes. At her short nod, he continued. "I can't wait to get started. I promise you, Della, I will give it 100 percent." The earnestness in his voice convinced her, sending her spirits soaring.

"If that's the case, then I have something for you to consider."

He regarded her quizzically for a moment. "Great. I'm listening."

She told him about the historical society and explained about listing the house in the National Register of Historic Places. Not once did she mention it as Daniel's idea.

"They don't buy the place or maintain part ownership?"

"No. They check court records and pinpoint the exact year the house was built. They tell you how to evaluate the historical value and suggest ideas for making or keeping it authentic. By registering, you become available for grants and sometimes they even help with maintenance. You can open it to the public or not. But, here's the clincher. We can register it, but they are the ones that approve the registration. Without their approval, no state grants or fees will be awarded."

"What would that involve?" He stared back at her in waiting silence, his interest apparent.

He placed his hands against hers, measuring the difference in size, then intertwined their fingers. She seemed to be drifting along on a cloud and had to restart her explanation several times, so weak in the knees, she needed to sit down.

She moved to the chairs in front of her desk. He followed, holding captive one of her hands.

"They have a certain amount of say in what needs to be added or removed from the premises. For example, glass and chrome appliances or tables would be too modern. Marcelo's swimming pool would definitely not work." They both chuckled at that, knowing and loving Marcelo and Kayla's cross-shaped pool with a convenient hot tub nearby.

"The Queen fits the bill perfectly, then. Everything we possess is older than we are."

He looked around the office. "Even the paint."

"Painting this room is on my to-do list. Just haven't decided on a color yet."

He let the comment pass.

"So tours would only be on the days we chose and only as many times a month as we want, right?"

"Right."

"And we set the individual and group prices?"

"As far as I know."

He stood and strode to the door. His voice rose with excitement. "I can't believe this money pit could be what grants us a ticket out of bankruptcy and poverty. With the money we make here and from the orchards, we can finally have a life. I'll get started on remodeling. We can't do much till we get our hands on some cash, but water and elbow grease go a long way. Get those people here, Della, as soon as you can." He thought for a moment as if he were going to say something else, and then the door closed quietly behind him, leaving her with an inexplicable feeling of emptiness.

Chapter 8

Adele pulled the slanted-edged trim brush along the top of the wall, careful to avoid touching the ceiling. Eight o'clock at night was not the best time to start a job like this but if she kept busy she didn't think about a sorry low-down rascal named Raoul Fuentes. Five days. Five. She'd seen neither hide nor hair of him. All those promises. *I'll give 100 percent.* Right. And she owned a condo at South Padre Island.

She couldn't decide who she was more disappointed with, him or herself. She must have been desperate for hope to believe his words. One good thing had come out of it, though: she had gained her momentum back and accomplished so much even her dad had remarked on how good the place looked. She set her timer each day, working an hour on one project then switching to another when it went off. And she loved it all. The office work proved the most challenging and she'd found several areas in which to save money—had actually found a loophole in the retirement insurance. They were still paying premiums for a person who'd been deceased two years. The reimbursement from that little mistake would soon put an amount in the hacienda account balance that hadn't been there in years.

She'd liked to have shared that with Raoul, but he'd not slept in his bed in a week. She'd texted him, called him, even driven the golf cart to the orchards. No one had seen him. She would have filed a missing person report, but this had been a common occurrence the past four years. At the end of the month, she would receive the credit card bill from whatever hotel he'd been to. Such was her life.

She leaned back on the ladder and studied her work. Berry-berry was the paint color and she loved it. Just a few more feet and the upper trim would be finished. The walls would be easier and more quickly painted with the roller; what little walls showed in the library as most were covered with bookshelves. This was her favorite room in the hacienda. Raoul's great-grandpa had added it to the original house in the early thirties. There was no second story above, so the walls were twelve feet instead of the standard eight that were in the rest of the hacienda. It had two trey ceilings with shaded skylights which allowed natural light to bathe the bookshelves without excessive heat or sun rays. Ornate moldings and dormer windows added to the beauty and even the peeling paint and rotted wood had not taken away from its ambience.

Her dad had replaced the ruined moldings and baseboard when he returned from his fishing trip earlier in the week. Adele's buoyant mood had rubbed off on him. Though they weren't out of the woods financially, funds were available for materials if they did the actual work themselves. Her dad had bought what he needed from the flea market in the nearby city of Pharr. He'd even bought her paint there and she'd taken the expensive kind she'd bought back to the store.

She climbed down the ladder and headed to the laundry room to wash the paint from her brush in the utility sink. Who knew painting could be so much fun? And therapeutic?

"Anybody home?"

"In here," Adele answered Marcelo.

"I smell paint."

Excitedly Adele showed him the rooms she'd painted. He whistled his approval at the family room and library. "Who replaced the old wood?"

"Dad did. He bought it at the flea market, believe it or not."

"Joe did this?" Intense astonishment could be heard in his voice. "I thought he only knew how to work a computer."

"Yeah, well, a computer has Google, and the man loves a good search engine."

Marcelo laughed. "I'd like to have seen this."

Her sense of humor took over and she laughed with him. "I had to leave the room. He had a crowbar prying the old wood off. I just knew he would do major damage, but he actually did a good job."

Marcelo walked the length of the room, inspecting the repair work. "Did Raoul help?"

"Ha." Her voice was dry and cynical. "You're joking, right?" She sat on an ottoman and watched for his reaction. He grimaced.

"Well, surely he likes it. Maybe seeing it look this good will light a fire under him."

A warning voice whispered in her head. Kayla had said that Marcelo thought Raoul was doing a good job. Did he, too, think like Kayla that Adele needed to give Raoul a break? For the first time in her life, she was uncertain how to respond, so she remained quiet.

A probing query came into his eyes as he looked at her. "What's going on, Adele?"

"Raoul's not seen it." She might as well tell him, he'd find out soon enough. "He's not been home this week."

"Where is he?" Marcelo stood with his arms folded across his chest, feet apart, a definite change in his attitude from when he'd first entered.

"I don't know. No one has heard from him. There weren't any business appointments. The workers haven't seen him." She shrugged her shoulders. "I'm pretty much through worrying about him, Marc." She unwittingly used the shortened version of his name. "I have to move on. Figure out if The Queen has a place in my future."

His eyebrows shot up in surprise. "Don't be ridiculous, Adele. You love this place as much as the rest of us. More actually. You can't give up now. You're finally accomplishing the things you've wanted to do for years."

"Marcelo, I can't babysit your brother for the rest of my life. Not even for The Queen." She swallowed down the threatening tears. She had turned into a veritable water fountain. Twice in less than two weeks she'd been brought to tears. "I want what you and Kayla have…and Juan Antonio and Carina." She rubbed a finger along the welt of the ottoman, unable to look him in the eye. "I need freedom to make the right decisions for myself. I don't want my love for this place to cause me to miss the love of a good man."

He came close, looking down at her intently. "You're talking about Daniel Jacobs, right?"

"Maybe." She lifted her chin, meeting his gaze head-on. "I don't know."

Her reaction seemed to amuse him. He sat down in the chair closest to her. The sun had gone down but dusk was still an hour or so away. "Kayla said the two of you went on a date the other night."

"It wasn't a date," she explained exasperatedly. "A horse had been shot and I went with him on call. We grabbed a sandwich at the drive-through and came home."

"But Kayla said you didn't get home till after 2 a.m. and then you went somewhere with him the next day."

Adele had not known Kayla was such a talker. She would have to watch what she said from now on. Guilt whispered a reprimand in her ear. Kayla only talked with her husband. She was a true friend.

"The horse didn't even fall over. A steady stream of

blood flowed from his shoulder and Daniel patched it up. It was so pitiful, Marcelo. The horse stumbled sideways and propped against Daniel till he gained some strength. Daniel finally gave it a shot and he and the owner eased the big fellow down. It was so interesting to see him at work." She could hear the excitement in her voice but didn't care. "We went back the next day to check on him and there he stood in the pasture, not moving too swiftly but alive and improving."

"You sound very impressed with Daniel."

"I am impressed. He has a great work ethic. He's kind and considerate and fun to be with. And he likes being with me."

Marcelo eyed her with a calculating expression. "All the things Raoul is not, huh?"

Adele drew a deep breath and forbade herself to back down. "Pretty much."

He laid his head back on the chair and stared at the skylights. "You know, Adele, I never thought you an unfair person, and Lord knows we've all had our share of aggravation with Raoul, but in this case I'm a little disappointed in you."

Her mouth dropped open. She merely stared at him tongue-tied.

He gave her a sidelong glance. "You wanna know why?"

"Yes," she squeaked out.

"Because Raoul used to be fun and you know that better than most. But the workload here has turned him into an old man and old men are too tired to have fun."

"Have you hit your head, Marcelo?" She jumped up

from the ottoman, determined to give the man a fight if that was what he wanted. "You 'better than most,'" she mimicked his own words, "know he has never once completed a job around here, and Dad and I always have to pick up the slack."

"Do you not know why he's like that, Adele?"

"Yes, I know. Because he is lazy, petted and spoiled. He thinks only of himself, Marcelo. He promised me just last week that he was going to start giving 100 percent around here, but where is he while the work is being done. No one can find him." And her heart had died a little every day he hadn't shown up.

"Who did the new fence around the estate office?"

"He did?"

"Is it finished?"

Grudgingly Adele nodded.

"Who secured the new Alaskan contract?"

She could give tit for tat if he wanted to go this route. She placed her hands on her hips in an aggressive stance. "Who started to repair the orchard pick lift two weeks ago and never finished it? And the driveway potholes? Or how about the clothes dryer that's been sitting on the back porch so long we've stored stuff inside." When the words started she couldn't seem to stop. "He. Never. Finishes. Anything."

"Sit down, Adele."

She was too startled by his suggestion to offer any resistance. He continued in a tired voice. She'd never seen him like this.

"Which was more important? Getting Daniel's office ready, or the lift?" When she didn't answer, he continued. "The office. We won't need the lift till harvest time." She started to say something but he held up his hand. "He started filling the potholes the day you graduated. He stopped to come be with you. The next day the Alaskans arrived. Since then, it's been one thing after the other. There have been no breaks for him—not to have fun, nor to be with you." He swiped an impatient hand through the air. "And you have two other dryers that work, Adele, so that was not a priority, either." He sat up on the edge of the chair. "But just like you, short stuff, he's had issues dating all the way back to childhood that have made him into the man he is today."

She decided to let the remark about her issues go, rather choosing to ask what his words brought to her mind. "But there are other things, Marcelo, and you know it. He never takes anything seriously."

"Is it any wonder? Think, Adele." He began to pace the room. "How many times did Dad promise us he would take us fishing, then never showed up? Or Mom would plan a family trip and then go off and leave us with your dad?" Adele remembered all the times she had comforted Raoul and talked him out of being sad. The many times she had cheered him up by playing the piano.

Marcelo held his hands out in an appealing manner, then shrugged. "Juan Antonio and I acted out. We got into all kinds of trouble. We were mad at the disappointments and we wanted Mom and Dad to know. Raoul, on the other hand, chose not to be affected. If things worked, they worked, if they didn't, he'd walk away. His favorite saying is 'get over it…'"

"Or get therapy." Adele finished the sentence for him. Marcelo had stopped pacing and stood looking out over the front lawn. They were both silent, each lost in thought. Finally Adele asked a question that had been on her mind a lot lately. "So you think I should cut him some slack. I get that. But how do I get him to do anything around here?"

"A woman can pretty much get a man to do anything she wants him to."

Adele and Marcelo both turned to see her dad standing in the doorway. The Lord only knew how long he had listened to their conversation. "Is that right? And exactly how does she do that?" Adele tried but failed to keep the sarcasm out of her voice.

Her dad entered the room and picked up a book that lay on the table by the chair Marcelo had used. "Encouragement. Works every time." A man of few words he turned to leave, then delivered a pointed zing. "Nothing uglier on the face of the earth than a nagging woman who continually points out a man's mistakes." At the doorway he turned back and looked directly at Adele. "Maybe you could practice encouragement when you take Raoul some homemade peanut butter cookies and a tall glass of milk. He's almost finished remodeling the gatehouse opposite the estate office."

Her voice hoarse with mixed emotions she asked, "Why on earth didn't he come home at night?"

"Didn't want interruptions till he finished the job. Something about promising you 100 percent."

Adele sank down on the ottoman; a tumble of confused thoughts and feelings assailed her. She heard sounds and must have nodded because when she fought through the fog, Marcelo had gone and she was alone.

Like an automaton in the kitchen she stirred eggs, sugar and peanut butter together and dropped spoonfuls on a baking sheet. She set the timer, then raced up the stairs for a quick shower. She left her curls wet; her hair would have to air dry. The oven timer dinged and ten minutes later she climbed on the golf cart and headed to the gate.

Chapter 9

Raoul sat on the floor, his thoughts grim as he looked around him. He'd devoted a week to repairing the old carriage house, turning it into a paying entrance. Six turnstile lanes had been added along with a narrow desk with credit card computer terminals. The roof was finished, new wood cased out the windows and he'd just finished laying ceramic tile. He'd never wanted to walk away from a job so bad in his life. His knees were almost raw and his back would never be the same. And the place wasn't finished. Wiring and painting would require another full week of working round the clock. He didn't have another week to give. He had other obligations— an orchard to oversee. He couldn't afford to leave his fruit unattended because the sale of his fruit was their main income.

The packaging house needed to be cleaned of mold and the equipment needed a few minor repairs but there were only so many hours in a day. He'd had to hide out to do this job without interruptions and still he wasn't going to make his self-imposed deadline. He needed more time. He was sick and weary of the dull ache of foreboding that shadowed him every waking moment. The outer door opened. "Back here, Joe," he called out.

"Raoul Fuentes, what have you done?" Adele walked through the door, carrying a red-checkered picnic basket. So much for surprising her.

He didn't answer, just sat dejectedly on the floor, dreading the criticism he was sure to receive. She walked over and stood looking down at him. He didn't have to wait long.

"You look awful." She sat beside him.

He started to get up but she placed a hand on his arm.

"There's a chair in the other room. Let me get it," he offered but she shook her head, instead stretching her legs out in front of her on the floor. His stomach growled. She smelled of sweet perfume and peanut butter. They looked at each other until she bit her lip and looked away. With a pang, he realized she was nervous. His confidence took an upward turn. Had he not been so tired he might have jumped for joy.

"I brought you homemade cookies and a jug of milk."

"Peanut butter."

"Yeah. How'd you know?"

"They smell wonderful."

She opened the basket and removed the cookies and milk. He took them from her and dug in as if he'd not eaten in days. She watched him with a half smile on her face. He wiped the milk ring from his upper lip and grinned. "Like old times, huh?" He bumped her shoulder.

When he'd left her the other day, he'd been on cloud nine. She had finally, it seemed, accepted the adult version of him. He had despaired of it ever happening. He had loved her since he first set eyes on her. Granted, it had been puppy love, but his heart had only ever had room for his Della. But hard times worked against them, and he'd sown a few wild oats out of pure frustration. He'd begun to hate the money pit that stole so many happy times from him. And Della loved it with all her heart. A wedge separated them, the distance as wide as the gulf.

But the same object that divided them, he hoped, would pull them back together. He would do his best to make it happen. And she'd made him cookies. The first time in years. That had to be a step in the right direction surely. But experience had taught him to beware of Della's anger and often judgmental attitude where he was concerned. Tonight he felt he couldn't take it; it would be the last straw. He looked into her beautiful eyes and her expression was tight with strain. She looked away swiftly, leaving him with a terrible hollow feeling.

Adele smiled and looked around them. How on earth could she encourage him? How did she not nag? The place had been totally revamped. Who knew the cost of the repairs much less the desk and metal turnstiles?

He was spending money they didn't have. They would never be able to pay their way out of this. Why did he always do the wrong thing? What had he been thinking? Anger clawed at her like talons. She struggled to find sense in what her dad had said compared to the disaster this expense would mean for The Queen. A warning voice whispered in her head, *Nothing uglier than a nagging woman who continually points out a man's mistakes.*

"Della?"

She heard the uncertainty in his voice and it reminded her of when they were children and he needed her during an asthma attack. She'd been a kid herself and hadn't known how to help, but for some reason her presence had calmed him. How could a person love someone so much and yet not like them?

She looked at him and saw the old familiar guard was back up. He expected her to criticize, to be negative. She made a choice right then. If she lost it all, she would just go down with the ship. Treading on new water, she found herself in uncharted seas. "Raoul—" Her voice broke with huskiness, so she cleared her throat and began again. "This place looks fantastic. How on earth did you accomplish this in such a short time? And how did you know how to do all this?"

An almost hopeful expression settled on his face. She stood and walked to the desk, running an appreciative hand along the top. "This is magnificent. It has a fifties' design, yet it shines like new money." She blocked from her mind the cost of new furniture with an antique look. She imagined the amount was staggering to their swiftly dwindling finances.

"Look at it closely, Della." She heard a tiny shiver of expectation in his voice, and had no idea what he wanted her to see. She stared at the desk, searching for words that might please him. She liked his initial response to her feeble attempt at encouragement and for whatever reason, wanted to explore the feelings further. She walked around, noticed the shelves that had been hidden from the front side.

"I don't know what…" She stopped midsentence and let her fingers run over several small notches again. Then she bent and looked closer. She gave him a sidelong glance of utter disbelief. "No way."

"Yes, way." The childhood phrases slipped out automatically. A gentle laugh floated up from his throat. "That's the countertop Dad used in the packing shed." He joined her, his fingers moving over the same spot. "Remember how we tried to cut a piece of wood in two to make a swing seat and you said we could use Dad's Skil saw, that he wouldn't mind?"

"But you wouldn't let me. You were afraid I'd get cut. And it jumped out of your hands and cut grooves in the top of the table. It landed on the floor barely missing your foot." Then the shock of discovery hit her full force. "This can't be that table, Raoul. It was old and ugly, even back then." She hurried around to the front, taking in every detail: the stained color that caught the grain of the wood; the gleaming varnish. You could almost see yourself in the shiny surface. And it was free.

She felt her eyes widen with astonishment. "Wow. Did you do this?"

She truly admired the work, but what amazed her even more was the look of satisfied accomplishment on his face. Her praise seemed to have turned on a light inside him. She hadn't seen him this animated in forever. He showed her the roof repairs. On the inside was Sheetrock left over from supplies they'd stored in the barn after the last hurricane. The Spanish tiles on the roof he'd gotten from Marcelo, who used the same type when building his new home. He'd spent less than three hundred dollars on the entire project. She'd estimated the cost at about five thousand.

Her smile broadened in approval. "How did you know how to do this?" She knew he had never carpentered a day in his life, much less stained and varnished furniture.

"Your dad told me to look it up on Google."

She couldn't control her burst of laughter. "That's what he told me about painting."

They explored every inch of the place. Adele had never been inside before because the roof had sunk in several places and every grown-up on the place had threatened to whip the daylights out of them if they went in and got themselves killed. She remembered asking her dad if he'd really spank her if she were dead. He looked at her grimly and said, "Don't push it, little girl. You may never have had a spanking but you'll get one if I catch you even entertaining the idea of going in there."

"How did you get the nerve to come in here? Remember we thought someone died and was buried in here."

"When you told me about the historical society, I knew we would need to be organized for visitors, and that things needed to be up to code. I just know it will be a success, Della. Remember all our friends that wanted to come home with us just so they could see the 'hacienda'? We were used to this eyesore, but I knew it would be the first place they would make us fix." He took her hand so easily it didn't register at first. But her attention perked up at his next words. "And I wanted to jump-start our working together as a team."

She exhaled a long sigh. It had been a long time since she had felt this much peace and contentment. It just seemed natural to put her arm around his waist and lay her head on his shoulder. They stood thus for a few moments and then he turned her into his arms.

Her phone buzzed loud and long notifying her of a text message. Regretfully she pulled away. Then she started giggling. She shared the message with him.

Get your tail home now, little girl. Don't make me come down there. I'll give you both a whooping. @Dad

Six o'clock next morning, Raoul crawled out of his sleeping bag, his body weary and tired. But his steps were quick, confident and strong with purpose. Della liked his work. She had laughed and smiled, even held his hand. Had her dad not texted he might have stolen a kiss. He stopped in his tracks. Kissing was special. He shouldn't offer her a kiss any old place. He'd think up a special occasion, plan his moves just right so that it would never be forgotten.

He rubbed his hands together. He needed to work fast today. If he hurried, he possibly could get the walls painted—but three rooms and a bath? Not happening in a day. His friend Jayden would be here today to hook up internet and terminals and whatever else electrical they would need. Tomorrow was Sunday and he'd been brought up not to work on Sundays. He figured he needed the rest, anyway. But come Monday he had to get back to work.

He stuck his head under the bathroom sink and then toweled dry his hair. He pulled on paint coveralls and was ready to start rolling on paint when Adele called his name.

She carried the same red checkered basket of last night and he knew they were in for a good, tasty breakfast. Her dad strolled in behind her, his face an innocent mask, but Raoul had figured out during the night that Adele learned his whereabouts from Joe. He didn't care. His life finally had meaning and that it involved the money pit up the lane was even better. Mainly because Adele loved it so much.

They ate sausage-and-egg *taquitos,* and then to his utter surprise they helped him paint. By lunch he and Adele had finished rolling the walls in two rooms. Joe, who had kept his talent hidden, was an excellent trimmer.

"I'm going to the house to fix lunch. It's leftovers from yesterday, so cold fried chicken and potato salad, okay?"

"And bring the rest of that pumpkin roll Kayla brought over yesterday, will you?" Joe Rivas had a sweet tooth but it never showed up on his short slender frame. It wasn't hard to see where Adele got her height. The man wasn't an inch over five feet six and weighed possibly a hundred and twenty pounds at most.

She turned to Raoul, her gaze as soft as a caress. The tangible bond between them was back. He'd do everything in his power to keep it that way, but he still didn't know what to expect from this Adele. Would she stay like this or would one mistake cause her to revert back to bitter, dissatisfied Della. He watched the golf cart disappear up the lane and his heart already missed her, though she'd be back in five minutes with lunch.

"You seem chipper today."

Raoul looked at Adele's dad and suspicions set in. "Who told Della I was here?"

"I did. Was it a secret?"

"Actually, it was. I wanted to surprise her."

Silence reigned but when Joe next spoke, Raoul felt as if he'd been hit with a left hook. "Boy, you are so dense."

"You gonna explain that comment?"

"Why you wanna go off for days without telling her where you're at or what you're doing? Don't you know that she worries about you? Are you so uncaring that you enjoy adding to her grief?"

Raoul was astonished at the guilt he felt. He rejected it quickly. "You're joking, right?" At Joe's stern look, Raoul went on the defensive. "Have you forgotten how much she's despised me the last couple of years? The hurtful words, the awkward silences…for weeks on end. She chewed me up and spit me out. She acted like a cur dog. Always growling and biting, ready to fight at the drop of a hat. It was never ending."

Joe was quiet so long, Raoul tried to think of ways to clear the air. He didn't want to remember those things. He hoped he and Adele had gotten through them. Then Joe descended the ladder and leaned back against the long desk.

"Can you remember, son, when we first moved into The Queen?" At Raoul's nod he continued. "We had lost everything familiar. Our home. Adele's mother. I was grieving and had no idea how to raise a child, much less a little girl. She latched on to you and she loved The Queen. It became her security blanket."

Joe turned around and poured paint into the paint cup. He never uttered another word, just started to climb the ladder again. Totally exasperated, Raoul strode over and put his hand on the ladder. "Wait a minute, Joe? What does that mean?"

"What does a cur dog do when you try and take something from him?"

Raoul stared at the man who had quietly filled the shoes of his often missing dad. Comprehension dawned and his heart thudded in his throat. "He fights to keep it."

Joe suddenly seemed like the wisest man in the world. "Since she was six, she's not known a mother's love and though Marta tried, your mother had too many problems with your dad to ever give enough attention to her own kids, much less one that was not hers. Adele doesn't know the feminine frills nor the right way to treat a man, but I'd choose her any day to work beside me because I could trust that she'd have my back. She will never give up on anything. She's not a quitter. So unless you have what it takes to make her happy, to give her the security she needs, then leave her alone, son. Walk away. 'Cause if you do her wrong, I'll sever every tie I have with you."

Raoul's back ached. His muscles screamed. His whole body was engulfed in tides of weariness and despair. A voice inside mocked him. One thought barely crossed his mind before another followed. He had nothing to offer Adele but half-baked plans and promises. Not one ounce of security. He voiced his fears to his friend. "I can't provide for Adele. My wealth is tied up in orchards and a house that's falling down around our ears. And she deserves so much more. The best thing for me to do is walk away, to stay completely out of her life." His words seemed to lodge in his throat. He glanced at Joe but Joe's attention seemed drawn to something in the other room.

He took a deep, calming breath and willed himself not to cry. Finally he spoke through the huskiness. "But I can't. I tried leaving several times during high school but I missed her so much it was like a death. She's embarrassed me, cut me down in front of my brothers, even hid my own money from me. But I love her. I hate not seeing her. I always come home. I won't walk away. I will do all in my power to make her happy." When he went into the other room to finish painting, his hands were shaking.

Chapter 10

After lunch, Adele packed the leftovers in the basket, then donned her painting vest and went back to work. If her smile was too bright and her wit sadly lacking, no one seemed to notice. In fact, Raoul appeared pensive, not disturbed or angry, and her dad...well, he was just Dad. She had arrived back at the carriage house in time to hear a serious conversation between her dad and Raoul, a conversation she wished she'd never heard. She didn't stay to hear it all, but she'd heard enough.

"Slow down, girl. You're attacking that wall like it's on fire." Her dad took the roller and moved it in slow up and down strokes. She copied his movements and he continued with the trim.

Raoul worked fast to finish painting, and then when the technician arrived to install computer terminals, he left paint pan and roller without a word or backward look at Adele or her dad. He stepped into the main room, his greeting cheerful at best. Adele deliberately held her eyes opened wide, refusing the urge to cry.

"Well, that about does it."

Adele looked up. They had finished the second room in no time. "What about the restroom?"

"Raoul said he wanted the walls tiled so there'd be no graffiti. The tile and glue are in there and he'll start on that as soon as the terminals are finished. Not much we can do."

"Good. There's a lot I can do at The Queen."

As she headed to the hacienda, Raoul's words went round and round in her head: *I can't provide for Adele. The best thing to do is walk away.* Adele decided right then and there to never call the place home again. She would gather further information on how to preserve the place as a local historical landmark, then she would use her salary from Daniel to find a place to rent for herself and her dad.

At the hacienda, she kept the painting vest on and finished the library. The satisfaction she'd felt the night before was sadly missing.

"There you are."

Adele sighed loudly.

"What?" Carina spoke softly as if afraid of waking someone.

"There is no privacy in this house. People walk in and out without the common courtesy of knocking. Heaven forbid they should ring the doorbell."

"I'm so sorry, Adele. How rude of me."

Adele immediately felt contrite. "It's not you," she hastened to reassure Carina. "It's me. I'm an idiot."

"No, truly. You're exactly right. This is no longer the family home. This is yours and Raoul's and we need to be sensitive to that. It won't happen again."

"Ha."

Carina stiffened. "When I give my word, Adele, I keep it."

Oh, law. Now she'd offended her. Could this day get any worse? "I know you do, Carina. I was talking about this being my home."

Carina put a hand to her head as if battling a headache. "You know, Adele, you need to talk to a professional. You have issues that need to be addressed."

Breathe in, breathe out. Stay calm. You have no friends. No one is on your side. Be strong. Breathe in, breathe out. Adele picked up the paint pan and roller and carried them to the washbasin off the laundry room. She covered them with water to soak and washed her hands, letting the water run down over the tools. She sensed, rather than saw Carina enter the room behind her. She turned and walked by her, into the kitchen. In as calm a voice as she could manage she asked, "Would you like something to drink?"

Carina stared at her, a confused expression in her green eyes. "No, thank you. I have to pick Juan Antonio up in a few minutes. I came to invite you to lunch tomorrow after church. Kayla's serving leftovers at Confetti. She texted a moment ago and said she prepared way too much food for a *quinceañero* she'd booked tonight and for us to come help eat the evidence." She gave a halfhearted chuckle, her look still uncertain.

Adele picked up a paper lying on the countertop and fanned herself rapidly. Even with the air-con full blast, it was hard to cool the place on a hot midsummer day. Plus, she knew Carina's intentions. If someone Carina loved dropped out of church, she would kill them with kindness until they were restored and attending faithfully. Adele had now missed three or four Sundays in a row, as well as rondalla practice, nursery duty and visitation. So most likely when Kayla invited Carina and Juan Antonio to lunch, Carina, in turn, had asked if she could invite Adele.

"Not sure I can make it tomorrow. Maybe some other time."

"Adele, please. I hate to see you like this."

"Like what, Carina?" Adele made her voice soft and friendly, but to her own ears it sounded false. Carina favored her with a gentle, loving look that filled Adele with bitterness.

Awkwardly Carina cleared her throat, either in an effort for more time before she spoke or to gather her nerve. "Well, one moment you're extremely happy, then the next you're mad and take it out on anyone unfortunate enough to be close to you."

"We can fix the 'unfortunate' situation right now." Adele started toward the front door. "I believe you need to pick up Juan Antonio?"

"Adele, please don't be like this. You're my friend. I love you very much. I only want to help."

Biting her lip, Adele looked away. She couldn't bear

the hurt look in Carina's eyes, but the hurt in her own chest was too painful to bear. "I'm sorry, Carina. I've had a rough day. Seems like the odds are always stacked against me. I have nothing, yet everyone around me gets what they want all the time."

Carina pulled out one of the tall bar stools and climbed up, laying her crossed arms on the countertop. She nodded for Adele to do the same. "Tell me what you mean." To all purposes she had settled in for a long girl chat, but Adele knew she'd rather be with Juan Antonio. Who in their right mind wanted to hear all Adele's problems?

"What odds are you talking about, Adele? What's happened?"

Either Carina had the patience of Job or she truly did care about her, which increased the shame in Adele's heart. But the recent conversations with Carina and Kayla put her guard up and the free-flowing conversation of previous days was gone. Another calamity in her life. She must be related to Job.

"Like I said, Carina, I'm just tired. I'm sorry for snapping at you." She might as well get used to the fact that she could only rely on herself. "Where's Juan Antonio?" She started walking to the door. She might as well take charge of her life and that included never, ever letting anyone get close again. Like she knew she would, Carina followed her. A small sense of gratification soothed her frayed nerves. From now on, she would do what she could and it would be for her own good. The entire Fuentes family was on their own.

At the door, Carina surprised her by giving her a

tight hug. "Adele, I don't know what's troubling you. I wouldn't think it would be Raoul this time since he's working like a madman trying to fix things up in one week so he can get back to the orchards, but I know you have a heavy heart about something. So, if you can't or won't talk to me, please go see Pastor David. He is so easy to talk to and very private." She gave Adele's hand a gentle tug. "Please?"

Adele nodded, her throat too tight to speak. She watched Carina until her little car disappeared out of sight. Juan Antonio must be weakening. He normally wouldn't ride with her. His long legs didn't fit and he joked about sitting in the backseat. Wearily she climbed the stairs, ice spreading through her heart and soul. Her mind was languid, without hope. She pulled the covers over her. Her life was nothing but a bitter battle. That had to change.

"Where's Adele?" Raoul had twenty-five minutes to make it to church before the preaching service began. He could do it if he left this instant but he'd seen Adele's car still in the drive and wondered what excuse she'd give for not going this morning. Not that he judged; he'd been out a couple of times himself, but most of the time he was providentially hindered. Adele was not. And it wasn't like her not to attend. She was involved in every part of the ministry, but lately she'd been missing more and more services.

"I knocked on her door. No answer, so I checked. She's still in bed." Always a man of few words, Joe picked up his Bible, ready to leave.

Raoul hurried after him. "Is she sick?"

"Didn't say."

"Well, shouldn't you do something?"

Joe stopped and looked at him enquiringly.

"Take her temperature. Get her water…I don't know. Did you check her pulse?"

"She's twenty-three and I haven't checked on her in thirteen years."

"But—" Raoul was talking to the man's back. He put his hands on his hips in total frustration. Adele had missed church, yes, but she usually was working at something she felt needed to be finished. Not lying in bed. In fact, he couldn't remember a time when she'd ever been sick. Indecision ate at him. If he went to church, he could pray for her. Of course, he could do that here, but at church he could have others pray, too. He took the stairs two at a time and knocked lightly on her door. When there was no answer, he eased the door open a crack and sure enough she was under the covers, unmoving and quiet. He took a few steps into the room and watched to see if the covers moved. She took a deep breath and he sighed with relief. He backed out of the room and headed to church.

He thought of all he had accomplished with her help, not just yesterday but the actual running of The Queen. It still stood, mostly due to her loving care and administration. But in spite of all their hard work, the only way to save their home was with a huge cash infusion. Even if they turned it over to the government, the only way to survive personally was to move into a smaller home. If he could just get Adele to realize the unfeasibility of cooling and maintaining a thirteen thousand square foot house. Seven bedrooms with private baths, a huge ballroom with a mural of a place Raoul hated because it had taken his dad away from them. But even he had to admit the mural was stunning. And who in their right mind needed a formal dining room for thirty-eight?

They had closed off all of the rooms but the kitchen, living room and four bedrooms. They sometimes used the library and Adele had turned the sewing room into an office, but when not in use, the utilities weren't turned on. However, the air-con units were running only by the grace of God. They were dinosaurs. He prayed they held on until the fall harvest, and then they might be able to replace them one at a time.

He enjoyed the message by Pastor David and had almost made it to his truck when Marcelo caught up with him. "Come by Confetti. There's enough food to feed an army and we need to get rid of it."

"Adele's sick. I need to see if she's all right."

"Joe said he was going to check on her. Come on over and you can take them both a plate. If Adele's sick, she won't feel like cooking." Marcelo's persuasion made perfect sense, so a few minutes later he found himself chatting away to the new pastor. It was uncanny how much he looked like his brother, Daniel, and that distracted Raoul to a certain extent. He wasn't sure if he liked Daniel Jacobs or not.

But he had a few requests and a person should have enough confidence in the man of God to ask for prayer, he figured. It was new territory for him, but desperate times called for desperate measures, so when the pastor asked him how the grapefruit business fared, he jumped in with both feet. "We're in trouble. If you would wing a few prayers heavenward, I'd sure appreciate it." That seemed a bit selfish to him so he added sincerely, "If there's anything I can do to help you get settled in or with the church, just let me know. Me and the guys will be glad to help any way we can."

He squirmed as the pastor studied him a few moments. He felt like he had when he and Adele had been caught misbehaving. "There is something that might help us both out."

Raoul gave an anxious little cough. He'd done it now. Volunteered his men for whatever job the church needed done and they had no time as it was. When the pastor wasn't forthcoming with more info, Raoul managed a feeble, "Sure. What is it?"

"It's been my experience that businesses prosper when the owners give them back to the Lord."

"Yeah?" Raoul's interest was piqued, but his expectations were so low he doubted even God would help with the load he carried. "How does one do that?"

"Well, you know the story of Hannah in the Bible?" At Raoul's nod, he continued. "She asked God for a son, and when he gave her that son, she dedicated him back to the Lord. The Lord in turn blessed her with five other sons, and he also provided for Samuel all the days of his life. The application being that if God gives you something, give it back to him. Who better to take care of something than the owner, right?" He chuckled as if he'd told a great joke and moved away to greet someone.

All the way home, Raoul mulled over what he'd

heard. Could it be that easy? He'd never heard anything like that in his life. But wasn't that what had happened? He'd heard that story often enough in Sunday school that he didn't need to read it to know that was what happened, but when he arrived home that's exactly what he did.

According to her dad, Adele still slept. "So what's her sickness? Does she have a fever?"

"She said she was tired, to leave her alone."

"What was her attitude? Did she seem in pain or sad? Crying?" Raoul thought attitude had a lot to do with how quickly a person recovered from sickness.

Joe poured a glass of sweet tea and took the plate Raoul had brought from Confetti and settled in to one of the tall bar stools at the island. He said a few silent words of prayer and began eating.

"Well?" Raoul's sarcasm knew no limits with this man. He also knew Joe would put him in his place in a New York minute if he showed disrespect.

"Grouchy."

"What?"

Joe looked up with a vague hint of disapproval in his eyes. "Her mood."

"Oh."

Raoul leaned back against the sink and studied the toes of his shoes. Indecision ate at him. Adele had always taken care of him, shouldn't he do the same for her? He glanced up to find her dad had finished eating. They stared at each other across an awkward silence. Raoul had a foolish yet irritating urge to stare him down. He knew who'd be the winner, though, and felt frustration as the lids closed over his eyes.

"You got something on your mind, son?"

He shook his head. How did you tell a girl's dad you wanted to hold her in your arms and make her better? Joe stood to leave.

"Wait, Joe. Let me ask you something." One fault the man for certain didn't have was the gift of gab. Raoul quickly explained what the pastor had said about giving the business back to the Lord. "Have you ever heard anything like that?"

Joe considered a moment. "Nope, don't reckon I have."

"You think I should try it?"

Joe stuck a toothpick between his teeth and walked to the door of the kitchen. Raoul waited. He knew the man would answer if he wanted to and would not if he had nothing to say. That was his way. That's why Raoul and his brothers respected him so much.

"Couldn't hurt."

Chapter 11

Adele dragged herself from bed on Monday morning when the clock buzzed the third snooze alarm. She could not shake whatever had attacked her body. She felt lethargic and depressed, and had she not promised to help Daniel this morning she would have spent another day exactly as yesterday. Thirty minutes later, she sipped coffee as she crossed the huge foyer, down the back hallway that skirted the formal dining room to the last door, which was her office. She opened the wood blinds and flipped the computer terminal on. If she hurried, she could have the historical society booked with an appointment for later in the week. The rest of the day would be spent with Daniel, updating his contact list and tagging the farms with large animals. He wanted to key addresses into his GPS so emergency calls were found quicker and easier.

The woman at the other end of the line seemed bored and uninterested in helping Adele, which added to her already troubled spirit and aggravated state of mind. Still she agreed to send someone to register the information, not hiding her doubts that a place in South Texas could hold any historical value. *"Loca Mujer."* South Texas is full of history. Haven't you heard of the Alamo and the Rio Grande?

"Howdy, howdy." Daniel's voice boomed with happiness, good cheer and the eagerness of a puppy. But despite the moodiness threatening to make her day a disaster, Adele found herself smiling back at him. Who didn't love a puppy dog?

"Hey there."

He pulled the chair close to her side of the desk and sat beside her, checking to see what she was doing on the computer. His arm brushed against hers and she moved away slightly. He didn't seem to notice. "I thought I might catch you playing Candy Crush instead of working. No such luck, huh?"

"What's that?"

"A game of matches with a lot of twists and turns guaranteed to drive you insane."

She leaned back in her chair and looked at him with interest. "You play games on the computer?"

"All the time. You don't?"

She ignored his question, rather asking one of her own. "When do you find time?"

"I take time for all the things I enjoy doing. Work

should never be such drudgery that you don't enjoy life." He smiled with his eyes. Blue like the ocean, they reflected the humor so often hinted at by the half smile on his face. "You agree, right?"

"I think I do." At the curious lifted eyebrow, she explained. "In the last few years, I've not had time to even figure out what I enjoy. I mean, with college and The Queen, I never had time for fun."

He reached out, lacing her fingers with his own and pulled her up. "I think an illustration of how to incorporate fun and work is what's called for. Come with me."

She barely managed to grab her purse before he closed the door of his truck, safely locking her in. He had her key an address from his phone into the GPS that looked more like a Kindle. In seconds a map appeared with text directions as well as a moving arrow. It asked if she wanted to save the information, then provided cells to key in the name of the owner and how many animals he had, plus the current sickness and plan of treatment.

"Wow! Now that's modern technology."

He briefly smiled at her and waved at someone on the side of the drive. She looked up in time to see Raoul climb on the top of the gatehouse with a water hose. Her dad stood watching, his hands in his pockets, nonchalant as ever, as if Raoul couldn't fall off and break his neck. Before she could do more than gasp, the truck whizzed past, not allowing her to fuss at her dad or Raoul.

"You did that deliberately, didn't you?" She stared at his clean-cut profile. He had an air of authority and the appearance of one who if provoked might demand obedience or compromise from someone. That in itself was enticing, yet Adele found herself treading lightly, unwilling to give him any leverage to use against her. While it would be great to have someone make decisions for her and relieve her of unnecessary baggage, she couldn't imagine giving that much control to someone.

"If I had stopped, you would have spent the next thirty minutes scolding both guys and it wouldn't have mattered one bit. Both would have continued exactly as they were." An excited light was vivid in his eyes. "And for selfish reasons, I wanted you to myself."

"I can't imagine why."

He laughed, then stopped for traffic at the frontage road entrance. While waiting for an opening between cars, he gazed at her speculatively. "You really can't, can you?"

Adele had no idea what he meant, but she hated for someone to treat her as if she were a bit slow on the draw, so she batted her eyes at him and smiled. "Why don't you clue me in?"

He shook his head at her juvenile flirting attempt. "That was pitiful."

She placed a hand on her chest. "Tell me what you're talking about so I can quit this—" she made ditto hand gestures "—'pitiful' acting."

"I like being with you. You're an intelligent conversationalist, you're beautiful…a little too short for my liking but some spiked high heels might fix that…and you're a cheap date."

She kept her features deceptively composed. They pulled up to a brick ranch house and a tall figure came off the porch to greet them. Since he didn't turn the truck off, she guessed he meant her to stay put, so she did. In seconds he was back in the truck, following the man on his tractor to a back pasture. The next couple of hours flew by. Adele cataloged symptoms into the GPS thingy as fast as he reeled them off. They made three other calls, the last at Marcelo's place. The ranch foreman had called and left a message on the GPS and Daniel had to show her how to retrieve it. One of Marcelo's cattle had stepped into barbed wire and had cuts on its chest, legs and feet. It bawled loudly, its hooves dangerously close to Daniel's head. He applied salve, wrapped the leg and provided instructions for the cow to be put in a stokehold until the next day when he would return and remove the dressings.

Adele's hair was soaking wet from the heat and her clothes stuck to her. She wasn't an outdoors person, but this had been so interesting that she asked Daniel several questions of her own. He pulled into Dairy Queen and ordered them both bottled water and a chocolate dipped cone.

"Oh, I almost forgot." They pulled up to the hacienda and he came around the truck and opened the door for her. "Cheap?" She stood on the running board looking down at him, her eyes flashing. He looked so innocent but she knew the exact moment he remembered. He took her hand and helped her down, his grin infectious.

"Well," he drawled as they climbed the veranda steps

to the office door, "that is our second trip to Dairy Queen."

They both burst out laughing as they entered the office. Six people sat around the conference table, a plethora of different expressions on each face. But it was Raoul who stood and asked, "Della, where on earth have you been all morning?" He looked at his watch. "It's nearly one-thirty. You missed lunch and you almost missed the meeting." He muttered the last few words and sat down, embarrassed if the red in his neck was anything to go by. His black eyes were flat and as unreadable as stone.

Adele just then remembered the family meeting held the second Monday of each month. She always prepared lunch and the guys would sit around the island in the kitchen talking as they reviewed the budget. She often spoke her mind and none of the guys ever minded, but up until now, she had been the only female present. Even Marta had never joined them for the meetings. Today Carina and Kayla sat beside their husbands, a portfolio in front of each of them, and ink pens in their hands.

Just one more piece of evidence that things would never be the same. She looked at Raoul and he motioned her to the seat beside him. There lay the same green folder and ink pen but she was tired of the sham. It was all so hypocritical. She wasn't now—nor had she ever been—a member of the great Fuentes family and the sooner she accepted that little fact, the better.

"I feel a little weak." She looked at the faces of her friends and the only family she'd ever known and lied to them for the first time. "I'm going to go rest. Must have been the sun." She walked from the room, not even bothering to tell Daniel goodbye. She climbed the stairs to her room and locked the door behind her. A cool shower washed some of the fatigue away but clean water couldn't do a thing for anguish of the soul.

She sat on the bed and dreaded the next few hours. She'd spent the day in bed yesterday, had dragged herself out of bed this morning, and now it appeared she would spend today here, also. Someone tapped lightly on her door but she ignored it. Astonished, she heard the sound of a key, then the door swung open to reveal her dad. He closed the door, walked to the side of the bed and sat down. She glanced up at him but would not meet his eyes.

"Are you sick?"

She had never lied to him, even when she and Raoul were in trouble. She shook her head.

"I didn't think so." They sat in silence a few moments.

"There's an old saying in Spanish, *Fisgones nunca oyen nada bueno de sí mismos.*"

Adele waited. Surely her dad remembered she barely knew Spanish. But he looked at his hands clasped between his legs, then studied the door he'd just closed. Exasperated, Adele asked, "What does it mean, Dad?"

"Eavesdroppers seldom hear good about themselves."

Her mouth dropped open. He continued. "Next time you decide to eavesdrop, maybe you should hang around for the *entire* conversation. Not run away. Never took you for a quitter. Nor a slacker. But that's what you've

done and become these last two days. A whiny baby."
He stood and walked to the door. "Put your shoes on.
I'll see you downstairs in the office in five minutes."
Adele couldn't rally quick enough to protest.

She snapped her mouth shut, stunned by her dad's
bluntness. The door closed behind him and she sprang
into action. She slid on flip-flops, took the rubber band
from her hair, bent her head over and shook out the
curls. Her mind raced. Had Raoul added something important to the conversation she'd overheard? Had she
missed something crucial? She had no time to dwell on
answers to her questions. The one thought uppermost
in her mind was what her dad would do if she wasn't
downstairs in five.

She slid into the chair beside Raoul with a minute
to spare. Carina said, "Yay," and Kayla stated happily,
"Finally the voice of reason is here."

But the catalyst that brought tears to her eyes was
her dad. He walked in carrying a tall glass of lemonade and a pill in his hand. All he said was, "This might
make you feel better," and he dropped a Flintstones
vitamin in her hand, closing her fingers over it before
anyone could see.

"Sorry you've got a headache, Della. Hope the meds
kick in soon." Juan Antonio's statement was accepted
by everyone. Only she and her dad knew the truth.
She looked at him and he winked. She gloried briefly
in their shared moment and popped the vitamin in her
mouth. She took a huge swallow of lemonade. The vi-
tamins had to be over ten years old. But he had made
legitimate her lie about feeling bad. Their first experi-

ence together living a life of crime. And for some crazy reason, unclear to her at the moment, her dad's actions gave her joy. Made her feel loved. She opened the folder in front of her and uncapped her pen.

"We need volunteers. If you have time and can help in the next few weeks it would be appreciated." Raoul felt weary of the discussion with his family. The girls threw out ideas that hadn't been well thought out, and before he or his brothers could explain why they wouldn't work, they built them up until it seemed, to them at least, that the guys were shooting their ideas down without giving them a chance. "What we don't need are new ideas not yet proven and people who want a salary."

Worry gnawed at his insides. Something was wrong with Adele. The energy that drove her was missing and she appeared washed out. Not, mind you, that she wasn't still the most beautiful woman he'd ever seen, just the light had died out of her eyes. And the vitality she usually exuded concerning anything that happened at The Queen had changed to an aloof, I-don't-care attitude. She'd not responded with any suggestions or comments unless spoken directly to. What was up with that?

He watched Carina write something, then turned when Kayla spoke. Why had he listened to Marcelo's pitch about the women having good ideas that would help The Queen? All he needed, all he'd ever wanted was Adele's ideas. Because she truly had the good of the place at heart. As was evidenced by the comments from Carina and Kayla, they wanted the place to be a success because they loved the challenge, not the pre-serving of their home. Both ladies lived in new houses, beautiful places to start a home with four or five kids if they wanted.

"So basically what you need is a day of clearing out the attic and placing the more modern furniture in stor-age. We can use the antiques in the attic. And then you need our ranch hands and Juan Antonio's men to repair the equipment and paint the outside of all buildings as well as the inside of the packing plant and barn." Ana-lytical to the core, Kayla had gotten the gist of every-thing he'd presented. Had he been able to talk things over with Adele before this meeting, he wouldn't have gone round and round the mulberry bush; she would have written them in order for him and he could have done a professional job in presenting his case for help. But Adele had gone AWOL. Normally she was a stick-ler for routine and he could pinpoint where she was at a certain time of the day as well as what she was doing. But these past two months, she'd apparently thrown schedules out the window.

"That pretty much covers it. If Adele, Joe and I were to try and do all this it would take us months because life gets in the way with different issues each day. We don't have months."

"Adele, did you get in touch with the historical soci-ety?" Joe hadn't said a word until now which worried Raoul somewhat, because he usually kept them all out of trouble. So did his lack of communication mean he was for or against the idea?

"Yes, Dad. They will be here Tuesday of next week."

She rubbed her hand over the edge of the portfolio which still had nothing written in it. A sure sign she didn't agree with anything so far.

"That gives us six good working days." Juan Antonio slid his chair back. "I think we can accomplish everything in that length of time. The problem will be buying the supplies." He raised an eyebrow and directed his next question to Raoul. "You got it covered or do you need help?"

Raoul felt a hearty dislike for his family right now. Who asked personal questions in front of strangers? A tiny voice whispered there were no strangers present but to him the only people allowed to know the financial circumstances of The Queen were the people that worked to keep their heads above water. That would be Joe, Adele and himself. As far as he was concerned, his brothers and their wives could take a hike. A long one.

"It's covered." If he had to take out a loan he would do it. No, that wouldn't work. His brothers would have to sign the loan application. Frustration ate at him. Would he ever be rid of all the hoopla and interfering and be allowed to make his own way? How he wished Adele would just leave with him. He would disappear and never look back.

He watched as they all dispersed to different areas of the house—Joe most likely to his rooms, and the women to the kitchen carrying the empty coffee cups. He saw Carina slip an arm around Adele's waist and hoped things would smooth out there. He rubbed a hand over his stomach and wondered vaguely if he had an ulcer.

Chapter 12

"What's bothering you, sweet Adele?" Carina's softly spoken words soothed the painful, jagged edges of Adele's nerves and she felt a moment's relief from the confusion of the past few weeks. "And don't say 'nothing,' because I love you and know that there is something."

The family had joined them for breakfast this morning to get an early start on the repairs. Kayla beat them to the kitchen and began stacking plates and coffee cups into the dishwasher. "Are you okay, Adele?" she asked as they entered, a worried pleat between her brows as if she were squinting in the hot Texas sun.

"I have a few personal problems but nothing I can't handle."

Marcelo joined them and slid his arms around Kayla's trim waist. She leaned back against him but kept her eyes on Adele. "We're here for you, you know."

"Nope, we're not, short stuff. You're on your own." Marcelo drew back in defense as Kayla swung a playful hand at him. "I'm telling the truth. Alma just called and said Confetti received three catering contracts. Something about beginning-of-the-school-year parties for volunteers and teachers."

Kayla changed the raised hand to a fist pump. "Yes!" she yelled, then immediately looked contrite. "Oh, Adele, I promised to help you today."

"Go." Adele waved the two of them to the door. "Get out of here. I know you have work to do, Kayla."

Marcelo patted Adele's head as he passed. "Kayla rode with me so I have to take her back to the ranch to get her car. Tell the guys I'll be right back."

"Will do."

"Okay, girly. Looks like it's just you and me, so what're we doing?" Carina had worn knee-length cut-off jean shorts and a long sleeve shirt. She looked too young to be married.

They headed to the attic to see what pieces would be useful. The attic in this case consisted of two rooms at the back of the upstairs. The hacienda had a flat roof so there was no attic space to speak of. All unused furniture, paintings, vases and the like were stored in the rooms until someone dragged them out and used them again. The Christmas decorations were also stored here. Once, a long time ago, Adele had tried to organize the two rooms but that had proved nigh on to impossible.

Instead, she had cleaned the place and boxed what she could lift.

"You know what?" Carina blew the hair out of her eyes. "I think it would be best if we went through the other rooms to see what might be needed to give it a more historical look."

"Okay," Adele agreed. She grabbed her pen and notebook. "We need to coordinate the things we have with the things we need."

They started in the rooms at the far side of the upstairs. Eight bedroom suites with private baths. Each room included a small sitting area with a love seat, two small recliners with assorted end tables, a desk and chair as well as a queen bed with nightstands. There were no dressers or chests of drawers because the walk-in closets had places for folded clothing. Each bathroom had an old claw-foot tub as well as a shower but both were antique and often presented plumbing problems. Her dad said if the proper pipes were installed the problems would disappear, so Adele hoped to have that done in the near future.

Carina admired the ornate headboards and the moldings and baseboards. The tile floors were different colors in each room but the same design and matched to some degree. "This is an awesome place, Adele." Adele could hear the surprise in Carina's voice. "I've never been up here."

"You haven't?"

"No. I mean I've been to your room, but that's all." She tested her weight on the side of the tub. It shifted not one inch nor did it shake. "Does anyone ever use this room?"

"It hasn't been used in years. Guests slept in here when the Fuenteses from Mexico visited but that hasn't happened since Raoul's grandparents passed away."

They checked the other bedrooms including Ms. Marta's, Adele's and her dad's but Raoul's they left alone. She hadn't been in his room since he'd yelled at her in high school to stay out. He washed his bedclothes when he couldn't stand it anymore and his clothes were taken to a laundry service each week.

Carina propped her hands on her hips. "You mean to tell me there are four perfectly good, furnished bedrooms in this place that are never used? Five really, if you count Ms. Marta's."

"Yep. One day you and Kayla can fill it with little Fuenteses," Adele teased.

"I doubt I'll get my three extra bedrooms filled up, but this would surely be a great place for kids to visit Gramma. Not that Marta fits the role of Gramma that well." They both giggled. Marta's modern way of dressing tended to lean more to diva than Gramma. "How I wish my mother could see this. She would be blown away with the antiques in this place."

"You should bring her over."

"You wouldn't mind?"

"Carina, you're family. You have more authority in this house than I do."

Carina showed her disbelief in the tone of her voice. "Adele Rivas. How can you say that? This is your home. I've never thought otherwise. That's why we ask you if we can eat here or have a party. I can't imagine any other woman here. Even Marta doesn't fit as well as you."

"But I've never tried to make it seem like it wasn't your home, too. If I did, I'm very sorry. You don't ever have to ask about anything here."

"You've always made us feel welcome and you've never turned us down, but in my mind and heart, I'm conscious of the fact that The Queen is yours." She shrugged. "This may sound crazy, but she's yours, Raoul's and Joe's. I can't separate that. It just is."

Adele feared her uncertainties of the past months would cause her to say something that she'd later regret so she remained quiet. But she was afraid that Carina's suspicions that something wasn't quite right could be seen on her face as easy as day.

"Adele, have we made you feel that this is no longer your home?"

When Adele tried to speak, her voice wavered. "Not in so many words, no." She moved out of the bedroom. "I think the bronze sconces would look good with the sofa tables in there." She pointed to the room they'd just left.

Carina nodded but Adele could tell she wasn't going to let the subject drop. "Adele, how old were you when your mother died?" She hooked her arm through Adele's and slowed to a sedate stroll.

Adele wondered briefly if Carina's arm was holding her so she couldn't move away or if she wanted the closeness of friendship. Either way, it frustrated Adele because she was not in a confiding mood. Last night, she'd actually gotten excited about the things Raoul presented to his family and thought the changes just might work. And if the family helped, well…many hands made for light work.

"I was six, Carina. You've heard that story a thousand times." She turned to pick up the sconces and Carina let her arm drop. "Let's get a move on. Before you know it, we'll have to stop and fix a meal and that will cut majorly into our day."

"Okay, okay. I'll let it go. But will you at least promise me one thing?"

"If it is within my power, I will." Adele fell back on words she'd heard her dad say almost every day of his life because at some point or other during the day, she would ask him to promise her something.

"Promise me that you'll talk to Pastor David about all that's troubling you. You've needed to vent for some time now and having someone outside the family is just what the doctor ordered." She smiled at Adele, then pushed back a wayward strand of hair. "Alrighty, let's get moving. Sconces." She held them up and rattled off the style and the bedroom each was going into. Adele wrote it down and they placed them in a box to carry downstairs later for washing.

By the time they stopped for lunch they were hot, tired and dusty, but they'd accomplished more than Adele had dreamed they would. The guys talked very little through lunch. They smelled of sweat, outdoors and paint. Her gaze returned time and again to Raoul. His usually lively eyes were dull with weariness. Would he quit before the job was done? Disappear like he'd been known to do in the past?

The other guys laughed and teased each other, but Raoul sat quietly eating, lost in thought. She was torn by conflicting emotions. On one hand she wanted to comfort him, rub the tiredness from his shoulders; but on the other, she feared he would walk out and she'd have to clean up the mess he'd made. Carried away by her thoughts, she failed to notice he'd finished eating and was watching her intently. She caved under the heartrending tenderness of his gaze. Her feet moved of their own accord and she poured tea into his glass. Her hand shook just slightly.

While the others talked and laughed she gently touched his shoulder, trying to encourage, hoping to convey her pride in him. It had worked at the gate-house. She withdrew her hand from his shoulder and let it fall to her side. He reached out, lacing his fingers with hers.

She glanced around the table. No one could see their hands, but surely they heard her heart beating. No one paid them the least attention. She stood at the kitchen island beside him while he with both hands traced her fingers. Her dad asked for more tea and reluctantly she moved to pick up the pitcher. Raoul slid off the bar stool and had to squeeze between her and Marcelo's seat to exit. He lightly placed his hands on her waist to anchor her so she didn't spill the tea. Then he was gone. But the special feeling he'd inspired held her in its grip the rest of the day.

* * *

"You're gonna wear yourself out, man, before the job's halfway done." Juan Antonio stood with his elbow propped on a shovel, surveying the new fence they were erecting to keep visitors out of the orchard. Raoul was installing the gate so they could enter only single file. The last thing he needed was twenty or thirty screaming kids turned loose among his grapefruit trees.

He clenched his jaw and hammered the last spoke in the top pole of the chain-link fence. "We're almost finished with this job and the guys have completed the packing shed, so tomorrow we might be able to send your guys home for good."

His confidence knew no bounds. His body vibrated with new life. He was sure of himself and his rightful place in the universe. He was in love. Head over heels. He'd felt a strange, soothing comfort when she'd touched his shoulder in concern several days ago. He'd read shyness in her, but he'd read so much more. Her touch had reassured. She cared for him. He had only seen her briefly since then, but each time she'd smiled and waved.

"Are Adele and Daniel an item now?"

Raoul's stomach clenched and his gaze followed Juan Antonio's to where Daniel helped Adele onto the running board of his truck, then drove off. "She works for him." Raoul kept his eyes averted, hoping to avoid one of Juan Antonio's tirades about how he should take care of Adele.

"But where do they go every evening? And isn't she supposed to work on his files at the Queen office?

I mean, that is why we modified the gatehouse." Marcelo sounded slightly disturbed.

Raoul wanted to scream at him that *we* had done nothing to the gatehouse. Raoul and Joe had finished it by themselves. A wave of apprehension swept through him. It gnawed away at his recently gained confidence. So that's where she'd been this week. Her car had been parked in the usual place but he'd looked the house over and couldn't find her. Could she be interested in Daniel Jacobs? But Adele was the straightest shooter he knew. She would not string a guy along, would she? His determination faltered.

Juan Antonio spoke up. "Carina thinks it's good that she's seeing Daniel. She says Adele has been obsessed with Raoul too long. Maybe this will set you free, Roly Poly." Juan Antonio laughed, enjoying a childhood name Adele had given Raoul not long after she came to their home to live.

"Well, I don't want to be set free. In fact, I have no intention of letting her get away, so you can tell Carina to quit thinking. I will handle it from here."

"Whoa. Little brother's staking his claim, is he?" Raoul wanted to knock the derisive grin off Marcelo's face but he'd known the teasing would come, so he'd prepared himself. But Marc's next words poleaxed him. "I think that's the most adult thing you've ever done."

"Yep, you've finally grown up." Juan Antonio sighed heavily. "'Bout time."

"I've been managing this place for four years and you have the nerve to say that to me because I finally admitted I'm in love with Della?" He shrugged his shoulders in mock resignation. "You guys are nuts."

Juan Antonio pulled the bandana from around his neck and wiped his forehead. "You could have made it easier on yourself if you'd have realized it a lot sooner. Work gets done quicker when there's a team." He grabbed a water bottle from the cooler and chugged the bigger part of it in one swallow.

"Must have made you smarter, too."

"What do you mean by that, Marcelo?"

"Well…" Marcelo spread his hand to encompass the work they'd done. "Look at this place. More work has been accomplished in a week than in those four years." Raoul felt sure the aggravation he felt showed on his face because Marcelo's smile widened in approval. Nothing made his brothers happier than a good fight and though they hadn't actually resorted to fistfights in years, it didn't mean they wouldn't welcome one to let off some steam. "I'm just saying, Raoul, that you suddenly are thinking smart and it's a nice change."

Raoul's annoyance eased somewhat. "Well, the change is from the Lord, not Adele."

Juan Antonio perked up at that. "Yeah?"

"Yeah." He cleared the huskiness from his throat. "Pastor David told me to give the place back to the Lord. That He would take better care of it than me. I did it—" Raoul looked down at the ground, a bit embarrassed "—and it's happening right before my eyes."

"Our former pastor told me the same thing." Juan Antonio shared his experience. "When Dad died and I inherited his place in Mexico I had to stop work on my place here to go tie up ends over there. The sugarcane had just been planted and even though we had great field workers, I didn't have a foreman. I couldn't be in two places at the same time and I desperately needed the cash from the sale of Dad's place. The choices I had to make gave me permanent indigestion. Pastor Lopez told me that fear and worry were not pleasing to the Lord." He started loading their tools into the back of his truck.

"So what did you do?" Raoul never asked his brothers anything. He'd learned a long time ago that they thrived on revealing his ignorance about things. He would hear about it for weeks on end and then they'd drag it out for re-consumption at every family holiday. But he didn't care about this one. He was so thankful to God that it worked, that he wanted to shout it from the rooftops.

Juan Antonio placed two fingers over his eyes and grimaced before replying. "This was during the time I thought I had lost Carina." He waited until his emotions settled a little. Raoul noticed Marcelo had widened his stance, folded his arms across his chest and stared into the grapefruit trees, waiting for what Juan Antonio would say. "I refused to let God do anything for me. I mean why would I give God my business when He denied me the one person I loved with all my heart and soul?"

Raoul remembered vividly the wreck Juan Antonio had been when he returned to the States. He was like a bear with a sore paw, and the light in his eyes had died. It had been horrible to witness.

"But God brought her back into my life, remember?

When you couldn't get the grapefruit trucks through the checkpoint?" At Raoul's nod, he continued. "I felt hope for the first time in six months. But I knew I couldn't be happy till I made things right with Him. I drove up the road to a rest area…" He paused, and Raoul swallowed hard. He knew the pain and confusion his brother had felt and the fragile hope suddenly within his grasp. He'd felt the same way the night he'd surrendered The Queen and his life fully to the Lord. He glanced up to see unashamed tears in Juan Antonio's eyes. Marcelo had turned his back on them, but Raoul watched him swipe at his face, then wipe his hands on his jeans. "I laid my head on the steering wheel and cried like a baby. I gave it all to Him that night—Carina, the business and my life. Since then, my blessings have far outweighed my trials and I never want to go back to carrying the load by myself again. I found my favorite Bible verse during that time."

"Yeah." Marcelo hooked his fingers in the back pockets of his pants. "What is it?"

"Romans 2:4. 'Despisest thou the riches of his goodness and forbearance and longsuffering—not knowing that the goodness of God leadeth thee to repentance?'"

The three stood quietly, each one trying to gain some sort of control. Finally Raoul felt he could speak without making a blubbering fool of himself. "It works." He pointed to the project they'd just completed. "A little over three weeks ago, this would not have been a possibility, but through His goodness, He has provided."

Marcelo threw his shovel into the back of the truck with Juan Antonio's. "Well, don't go counting your chickens before they hatch. The jury's still out on who Adele will choose. You or Jacobs."

Yep, Raoul thought, *we're back to normal. Bonding moment over.*

Chapter 13

Adele paced the floor in her room, determined to fix her life and rid herself of all the negative thoughts and fears that tormented her. Enough was enough. She'd been angry most of her life. First at God for taking her mother. Then at her dad for blocking her out of his life. Until recently, they'd never had a personal father-and-daughter moment. She'd resented that and felt cheated. Now she fought for a home that wasn't hers, she loved a man she'd heard with her own ears say he had nothing to give her; in fact, she'd wasted so much love that she had none left to give.

And what had her dad meant the day of the family meeting by that little saying about eavesdroppers? She kept meaning to ask. And how had he known she'd overheard Raoul in the gatehouse, anyway? She'd exited as quietly as she'd entered, loudly announcing herself when she returned some five or so minutes later.

Then the other day, she'd shared a private moment with Raoul, much like the day he'd promised her 100 percent cooperation in saving The Queen. He'd called them a team. And he'd touched her gently and held her hand. What did it all mean?

She hated the miserable person she had become. Her relationship with Kayla wasn't the same as it had been in the beginning; and her dad suddenly felt it necessary to correct her and guide her. Really? She'd been an adult since she entered junior high. She'd been forced to be one, while Raoul lived life to the max. Her youth had been stolen and she had become bitter, mean and spiteful.

So where did that leave her? Where did she go from here? She was sick with the struggle within her. She wanted to do good, but her anger and disappointment in others as well as in her life always won out. She put her hands in her hair and pulled. "Aiiiii," she said aloud. "I need help."

Promise me you'll talk to a professional. Carina's words whispered through her head. Adele grabbed her phone, made an emergency appointment and ran to her car. Desperation drove her. When she reached the church office she wasted no time on pleasantries. She unloaded all the lonely days of decisions and failures onto Pastor David's shoulders.

"So basically, Adele, you're scared of what the future holds because of past experiences?"

Pastor David made her problems sound so simple

and he'd gotten it in a nutshell. She started to say something but he continued. "Let me finish, please." His words brooked no argument but the kindness and concern in his eyes impressed her and inspired her confidence in him. Carina had been right. She'd needed professional help.

"May I ask you a personal question?" She nodded and he asked, "Have you invited Jesus into your heart?"

"I guess."

He studied her a moment, then seemed to reach a decision. He crossed to her side of the desk and pulled the Bible forward for them both to read. But before they started, he prayed that God would open her eyes and heart to receive what she needed. He then walked her through the plan of salvation. She'd never seen it this way. She tried to explain to him that she'd always believed there was a God and that was all it took to be saved. He showed her Scripture that said the Devil also believes and trembles. When she finally grasped that it took a personal acceptance and invitation from God to come to Him, her heart became so heavy she found it hard to breathe. She was lost. She needed a Savior.

All these years, she had been alone, trying her best to carry all the burdens of those around her and time after time she had failed. Her life had been filled with never-ending turmoil and there had been no one to help. She felt as if she stood on the edge of a precipice. If she fell, she would be in darkness, pain and despair, but if Jesus would save her, she'd finally be loved with an everlasting love. She felt drawn by the gentle pull of the caring Lord and her heart cried out for forgiveness. Peace so overwhelming and sweet filled the dark shadows of her soul, healing and restoring all that was sick or lost. Great gulping sobs shook her body. She experienced humbleness and joy and a fulfillment that had never been there before.

Finally she looked at Pastor David and tears marked a path down his face and still lingered on his eyelids. "The Lord just saved me, didn't He?" Though she asked the question, no one would ever convince her to the contrary. She knew it with perfect assurance.

Pastor David shared several Scriptures with her that strengthened and added to her knowledge, and he explained the next steps she should take. They made appointments for new convert classes. She left the office and met her friend Alma on the sidewalk. Before Alma could say a word, Adele blurted out, "I just got saved."

Alma seemed stunned for a moment and then she squealed and grabbed Adele in a fierce hug. They sat on a bench outside the sanctuary and Adele told her all that had happened. Alma cried with her and told of her own salvation experience. "I can't explain it, but I feel lighter," Adele said in wonder.

"You are lighter, my sweet friend, now that all your sins are gone. Sin weighs us down."

Adele exhaled a long sigh of contentment.

She arrived home just as Daniel was leaving.

"What's happened?" He stopped midstride when he saw her face.

"Why do you ask?"

"You're glowing." He considered her a few moments. "I don't think I've ever seen you look so happy before."

"Pastor David explained the Scriptures and I asked the Lord into my heart."

"That's fantastic," he enthused, giving her an awkward hug. "I thought you were already a Christian."

"I did, too, but when he explained the plan of salvation, I realized nothing had ever changed in my life. But now… Oh, Daniel, it's such a great feeling."

"It sure is. Did he enroll you in new convert classes?"

Surprised, Adele nodded. "Why yes, he did. For two weeks starting tomorrow evening at six."

"Would you like to ride with me?"

"You're going to the classes?"

"I'm teaching the class."

Her smile broadened in approval. "That would be great."

Adele watched him drive away. Daniel was such a good man; and a good friend, too. And now they had even more in common. He was her Christian brother. The religious terminology she'd heard all her life now made sense to her. And she'd been saved what? She looked at her watch. All of sixty minutes. Now that was amazing.

She sat at her desk in the office, determined to catch up with paperwork that she'd gotten behind on while redecorating the house. She forced herself to settle down. She yearned to play the piano. She could almost feel the keys beneath her fingers and hear the hymns Ms. Marta made her painstakingly practice until she mastered them. But she needed to record the visits Daniel made today and get the invoices ready to mail so he would receive payment for his services on time. It suddenly seemed imperative that she do things right.

The work seemed to get done with hardly any effort at all. Not only did she finish Daniel's work, she did the next day's payroll for the Queen's employees, then started cataloging the items in every room. The historical society had emailed her several papers to look over before their initial visit and an inventory list was required. They would make their own, but compare Adele's list with theirs to make sure nothing was missing. She frowned and wondered for the umpteenth time if she and Raoul were doing the right thing. *You could ask your Heavenly Father,* a small thought whispered inside her.

The newness of her salvation delighted her and she bowed her head. As the words began to flow, she gained confidence and she poured her heart out to God, loving Him through his Son. Cleansing tears of joy ran down her cheeks.

"Okay, daughter. We need to talk."

She jumped in surprise and hurriedly wiped her tears away.

"What did you overhear the day you came to the gatehouse?"

The events of that day were so far removed from her mind it took her a few moments to gather her thoughts.

"I know you heard, because I stepped up on the ladder right before Raoul said he had nothing to offer you. I was looking out the window and you never came down the road from the house, which could only mean one thing. You were already in the outer room."

Her dad watched her, waiting for confirmation. "Yes, I heard him say that he had nothing to offer me, that the best thing for him to do was walk away."

"And is that why you've been moping around here the last couple of days with a chip on your shoulder?"

"Well, how would you feel, Dad, if one minute someone acted like they loved you and the next said they had nothing to offer and planned to walk away?"

He rubbed the crease in his jeans and she could tell he was uncomfortable with the conversation. A man of few words, he had talked to her more in the past three months than he had her entire life. At least it felt that way. "I reckon I'd feel pretty low, if that was all that was said."

"What do you mean?"

"You should have hung around a few more minutes."

That's all he offered and Adele, with her newfound peace and grateful heart cocked an eyebrow at him and waited. If he could use facial expressions and silence to get his points across, so could she. She hadn't needed or wanted this conversation today; her life had moved happily along, and though she knew she loved Raoul with all her might, a new love resided in her heart and she felt completely satisfied.

"It's true that he said he had nothing to offer and that he should walk away, but then he said he couldn't. That even though you were the proverbial pain in his backside, he loved you and he would do all in his power to take care of you."

Adele stared wordlessly across at him, her heart pounding. "Are you sure, Dad?"

But she knew he told the truth. He'd never sugar-coated anything nor uttered words of flattery to make her feel better. What a wonderful, wonderful day it had turned out to be. Just a few hours earlier she had been in despair; and then she had received the precious gift of salvation and now her love was returned by her childhood friend—her soul mate. Tears of happiness found their way to her eyes. But her news was even better than her dad's and she rushed around the desk to share it with him. Before she could speak, he stood up, his expression crestfallen; confusion evident as to why she would cry at his explanation.

"Dad, something wonderful has happened."

He drew back his shoulders and looked at her as if she'd lost her mind. "I thought you might feel like that, so why the tears? Can't stand a crybaby."

She placed a hand on his chest. "Dad, I talked to Pastor David today and I asked the Lord for forgiveness and to come into my heart. He did, and I am the happiest I've ever been in my life. Isn't that great news?"

He reached out and pulled her into his arms, rocking her gently back and forth. "I'm happy, Adele. Very happy."

The next day, Adele wiped sweaty palms down her skirt, tension mounting behind her temples. They'd been touring the house for almost two hours while the historical society documented and recorded all the facts she presented to them. Kayla texted her that refreshments were ready to be served in the kitchen.

"If you're through for the moment, my friend has prepared a snack and drinks, and then we can finish up in the office." As they followed her downstairs Adele let go of the frustration she'd felt watching strangers attach monetary worth—or lack thereof—to the things she thought of as precious heirlooms. If she heard the words 'oh, that's hideous' one more time she might scream.

Raoul came to the door of his study as they circled behind the stairs on their way to the kitchen. He raised an enquiring brow at her and she waved a finger at him, letting him know she'd be right back. She made sure Kayla and Carina would entertain the visitors and she all but ran back to Raoul. She closed the door behind her and leaned against it.

"What is it, Della?" The concern in Raoul's voice undid her and great big tears filled her eyes and rolled down her cheeks. She was abruptly caught in his arms, his hand rubbing her back in an instinctive gesture of comfort. Overwhelmed by the torment of the past couple of months and her emotional day yesterday, her fragile control broke and she cried her heart out, her tears soaking the front of his shirt. He murmured sweet nothings, held her tighter and finally pulled her to the window seat where they could sit side by side. He offered her a box of tissues and she blew her nose and wiped her eyes, shredding the tissue into tiny pieces. Finally she gained the nerve to look him in the eye and only by strong resistance did she maintain control of her emotions.

"They hate The Queen, Raoul."

"What did they say, sweetheart? Did they insult you?

What did they do to make you cry? I can have them out of our house in minutes."

How she had needed to hear those words from him. It was one thing to have her daddy verify what her heart longed to hear, but a different thing entirely coming from Raoul himself. A soothing balm began to heal the past pain of her wounded heart. Like water in the desert, she began to feel nourished and loved. Raoul would defend her. She knew that now as certainly as she knew her name. And he had called it *their* house.

"They keep saying things are hideous and one man said the furniture in your bedroom came over on the ark."

To her horrified amazement, his lips began to twitch. He bent his head and studied their hands. He pressed his lips together but his shoulders shook and she finally saw the humor of the situation. She smacked at him playfully, trying unsuccessfully to suppress a giggle. "I can't believe you're laughing."

Laughter floated up from his throat, deep, warm and rich. "I think it actually did come over on the ark."

"I know, but we're the only ones that can say things like that."

"If we go through with this, Della, there will be lots of changes in our lives. Are you prepared for that?"

She drank in the comfort of his nearness. The sound of his voice and the clean-air smell of him stirred a vibrant chord in her. Though she was by no means blind to his attractive features or his beautiful, strong physique, the thing that drew her most was how he made her feel. Like her happiness was important to him. As if he could not be happy unless she was. The wonder of it all was that just a few months ago they had almost despised each other.

She looked up to find his gaze riveted on her face. Her answer seemed very important to him, so she sought for the correct words to let him know how she felt. "When we are together like this and I feel like you value me not just for my opinion but as someone important to you, I'm ready to face anything that comes our way, even changes."

His soothing voice probed further. "And The Queen?"

She looked around his study, touched the ornate moldings of the window seat where they sat, then answered with the certainty of someone who finally had clarity on life. "I love this place to the moon and back, but if I had to make a choice between the person I loved and The Queen, I'd choose the person I loved." A few days ago, she would not have been able to say that, but having Jesus in her heart had shown her what was more important and it was not brick and mortar.

He leaned forward and kissed the side of her face, his cheek resting against hers. The door opened and Carina peeked in. If she was surprised to find them so, she hid it well. "They're ready for us. See you in the office."

Raoul regarded himself in the bathroom mirror. He'd needed a few moments before joining his family and the historical society. He saw a faint light twinkle in the depths of his black eyes. Excitement, eagerness and hope, too. She loved him. He felt it, accepted it and it humbled him. She hadn't said it outright, but she would.

He knew it in his heart. He'd noticed a gentleness about her just now that had never been part of her makeup before. She'd needed him; he'd comforted her. Never once in all the time he'd known her had she ever been willing to give up The Queen. One corner of his mouth pulled into a slight smile. God was good. All the time.

He entered the office and took his seat beside her. It came naturally. They would decide the fate of their home together. He reached for her hand and she placed it willingly in his. She trusted him to keep her best interests at heart. He would do just that.

Chapter 14

Rain pelted the roof above Adele's head and she snuggled deeper under the sheets. She loved the sound on the tile roof; she just prayed there were no leaks. The men had replaced several broken tiles when they'd done the repairs. Hopefully that was all that was needed.

The storm had formed earlier in the evening and she had been soaked running from Daniel's truck to the house. Last night had been the final new convert class and she would be baptized and join the church next Sunday morning. Church had become such an integral part of her life that she could hardly wait to once again sing in the choir and keep nursery. She had grudgingly participated in church activities before, always with a fake smile and the right words, but now they fed something inside her that gave her confidence and self-respect.

She drifted in and out of sleep. There was no reason to get up until later. The men fixed breakfast for themselves and she had all the office work caught up. The historical society had accepted their petition for the hacienda to be declared a historical house and was coming this morning to discuss the outcome of their inspection as well as the legal requirements and signatures. There were a few things they still wanted done before the lawyers finalized everything. The entire family would be here and she had a meal planned for them later so they could discuss the committee's requirements.

Unable to sleep anymore, she dressed and went downstairs. She carried a glass of iced tea out onto the veranda and stared at the water drenched backyard. Everything looked clean and smelled new. Much like when the Lord had washed her clean.

She hadn't spent any quality time with Raoul in the past week. He was catching up on the work in the orchards. Since it rained and the ground would be muddy, maybe he would be in earlier than usual. She needed to discuss so much with him before the history people, as Marcelo referred to them, arrived.

She strolled through the downstairs rooms, planning her strategy, trying to see the pros and cons as they had seen them. She chose the formal family room first. Her dad called it a ballroom, but it only seated fifty comfortably, so technically it was too small. The attraction of the room was the mural that covered the entire back wall, as well as the six floor-to-ceiling windows looking out over the back lawn and gardens. Her piano sat on a platform at one end and a cabinet podium hid the sound system. There could be nothing the society wouldn't like about this room.

The library was perfect in size and decor. The formal dining room still had the original table from the very first Mr. Fuentes: solid oak wood with thirty-eight matching chairs. The smaller dining room table was more modern but still dated back to the early 1920s. The kitchen boasted appliances that were old but not antique. The sewing-room-turned-office and the family room were filled with heavy oak handmade furniture. Raoul's study looked the same as it had when his dad lived here. There was the game room, but the only piece in it was a huge pool table with the felt worn in too many places to be of much use. And lastly, she studied the laundry room with the top-loading washing machines and dryers. Surely the dumbwaiter in the corner that had entertained her and the brothers for hours on end would count as an antique.

So many memories. Yet Adele had begun to see the place in a different light. In her talks after class with Pastor David, she had realized that fixation on an object usually resulted from a lack of confidence or from a sense of not belonging. Though her thoughts and feelings were not clear just yet, she knew the importance of the place had shifted in her life. Her beloved Queen no longer held top place in her heart.

She showered and dressed, then sat in the library and did her devotions. It started raining and the skies grew dark. She decided to prepare a light lunch because in storms like this the power often went out.

She heard the office door open and called out, "In here."

Carina and Kayla entered, their hands full of bowls and bags of goodies. Kayla apparently had robbed Confetti of leftovers. "I'm drenched," Kayla complained.

"It feels so good, though." Carina piled the containers on the island countertop. "The air has cooled down to low seventies. I wish I had brought a sweater."

"I know," Adele agreed. "It felt chilly in here till I started cooking. And this is just September. It usually doesn't cool down till the end of October or first of November."

Kayla towel dried her arms and hair. "It's because of the storms up north. A tornado touched down in Oklahoma. Did you see that on the news?"

"No, but Daniel told me about it. Death count at sixty-some last count. So very sad."

"So how's it going with Mr. Jacobs, Adele?" Kayla's voice teased but curiosity shone in her eyes.

While Kayla had been talking, Adele heard the door of the laundry room open from inside the garage. Only one person entered the house that way. Raoul. She'd heard his footsteps approach the kitchen but he'd paused when Kayla asked her question. She decided to have some fun.

"He is such a wonderful friend. I always enjoy being with him." She patted out the dough for a biscuit. She felt sure her ancestors would roll over in their graves if they knew she'd learned to make biscuits and not tortillas.

"So are you interested in him as a man?" Carina

stopped tearing lettuce and waited for Adele to answer. Adele winked at her and almost laughed out loud at the confused look on her face.

"Oh, yes. Can you imagine any woman not being interested in him?" She allowed a large dramatic sigh to escape. A thump sounded in the laundry room and both girls glanced in that direction. Realization dawned on Carina's face and she giggled. Adele shushed her. Kayla ignored them both and started to the laundry room to identify the noise. Adele and Carina grabbed her, hauling her back with a finger to their lips.

"I guess a lot of women would find him attractive." Carina sliced cucumbers and added them to the salad. Kayla looked at the other women as if they'd grown two heads.

"Would you consider marrying him if he proposed?" At Kayla's look of pure astonishment, Adele lost it and had to place the dishcloth against her mouth. Carina signaled Kayla that someone was in the laundry room listening to the conversation. Kayla raised her eyebrows and pointed. At their nods a huge grin split her face.

"Don't answer that, Adele. First you need to find out if he's a good kisser. You wouldn't want to marry a man that struck out on first base." Kayla thought fast on her feet.

Carina had a coughing fit, and Adele turned the faucet on full blast, the tears starting to run down her face. A shadow moved closer to the laundry room door.

Finally they got themselves under control. "Well?" Kayla prodded. "What's the verdict, Adele? Good kisser or bad?"

"I don't know," Adele answered truthfully. "He's never kissed me. I mean—" she paused for dramatic effect "—I want him to, but how do you get a man to kiss you?"

"Oh, I can tell you that." Kayla and Adele both held dishcloths to their mouths at Carina's declaration. One thing Carina would never do is participate in a discussion of that type unless it was pure fun like now. "This is what you do." She turned the mixer on and began to mumble. They watched the shadow move closer.

She turned the mixer off and motioned Kayla to follow her. "So let us know, Adele, if it works for you, okay? There's more than one way to get a man to the altar." They walked out of the kitchen and Adele braced herself for the fallout. She didn't have long to wait.

"What on earth are you thinking, Adele Rivas?" The hurt and anger in Raoul's voice sat at odds with the look in his eyes. "I thought you said you were saving your kisses for your husband. Now you're going to experiment and compare kisses?" He raised his voice. "And what kind of women did my brothers marry? I don't want you anywhere near them anymore." He hit the countertop with his hand. "Compare kisses. Who ever heard of such malarkey?"

"No one said anything about comparing kisses, Raoul. How can you compare when you've never been kissed? I said I *wanted* him to kiss me. I mean for pity's sake, I'm twenty-three years old. It's about time I experienced my first kiss, don't you think?"

"So you'd kiss a man just for the experience?"

"Well, I'd prefer my first kiss to be from someone

who cared for me, but I have a problem getting…" Adele shrugged, but her heart was beating in her throat.

Raoul walked toward her and she backed up against the sink. Holding her gaze he leaned to within an inch of her mouth. "I think I can handle that little problem for you and satisfy your curiosity, as well."

Then he straightened back up and called loudly, "But I don't plan on having an audience when I do so." A grin the size of Texas split his face and he flipped Adele on the nose. "Behave."

Carina and Kayla rounded the corner, sheepish smiles on their faces. They'd been had, but they also had accomplished something for Adele. They'd issued a challenge and she would reap the benefits. She could hardly wait.

The front doorbell rang. The historical society had arrived. She'd never felt more aggravated in her life. Ever the gracious one in the family, Carina ushered them in, taking their umbrellas, giving them hand towels to dry off with. There were five of them. Juan Antonio and Marcelo arrived a few minutes later.

They declined lunch and Adele all but groaned. She'd skipped breakfast and was starving. But she followed the rest into the office, anxious for the verdict. It didn't take them long to lower the boom.

"The Citrus Queen meets all the requirements for being listed as a historical landmark. However, there are some things we'd like to discuss with you." The man appeared to be in his early sixties. He cleared his throat loudly, sucking air through his throat to make a snorting sound. She froze. If one person so much as grinned, she would lose it.

"We would like for you to consider our suggestions before you give a definite answer, so today, because of the weather, we will tell you what we've decided and schedule another appointment for your decision after you've had time to talk about it."

He glanced at Carina who nodded her head in agreement. He appeared intimidated by the men and worried by Adele's tenseness and Kayla's obvious lack of interest. Adele imagined that to the committee, they were a very unusual bunch.

"Number one on the list is the parking issue. We think the cactus garden should be removed and the area cemented." He cleared his throat again. "Number two."

Adele's heart just about fell out of her chest. The cactus garden had been there since before they were kids.

"That won't be happening," Raoul stated in a no-nonsense voice. "Number two?"

One of the ladies looked as if she might argue but the speaker plowed on. "The mural in the grand room is too new. That causes the house to lose authenticity. We think it's beautiful, but it should be removed."

"Not happening." Raoul had things under control. Adele wanted to cheer.

This was too much for the lady who had tried to speak earlier. "But, son, you must make certain sacrifices if we're going to accomplish what you've asked us to do."

Very respectfully, Raoul looked her in the eye and

said, "Yes, I know." Then he looked at the speaker. "Next?"

The man started to clear his throat but Carina set a glass of water in front of him.

"There are eight bedroom suites upstairs, three of which are being used. Two are at opposite ends from each other. We advise using only one side of the house and making one of the bedrooms into a kitchen. That way, the downstairs will be preserved as well as your privacy."

"That one we will consider." Raoul leaned forward, calm as a cucumber. "Is that all?"

"Yes, actually, it is."

"So let me get this straight. You have only three suggestions. We've refused two of them. Will that hinder our chances in any way?"

"Raoul, don't you think we should discuss these things before you shoot them down?" Marcelo's voice held an edge of warning.

"No."

Adele watched the play of emotions between the brothers and knew Raoul wasn't budging. He reminded her of herself a few months back.

A clap of thunder broke the awkward silence and the group began to gather their things. Carina helped them find umbrellas and scarves and ushered them out the door. Kayla was on the phone to Alma at Confetti. Juan Antonio and Marcelo had walked to a private corner of the office and stood talking in low voices.

Raoul sat alone at the table. Adele walked back to him and took his hand and lightly pulled. He left his seat and followed her to the kitchen. She let his hand go and turned to tell him she appreciated his efforts. His head lowered and his lips touched hers like a whisper: gentle and light as a summer breeze. Raising his mouth from hers, he gazed into her eyes. She stared wordlessly back, the tenderness in his expression causing her knees to weaken. He wound a hand in her hair, his other circling her back. He tilted her head to better access her lips and then kissed her thoroughly, leaving no doubt of his feelings for her. He lifted his lips from hers. She kept her eyes closed for a moment, savoring his strong taste. When she opened them she said the first thing that popped into her mind. "Just as I remember."

He chuckled with happy memory. "Junior high. We were twelve. All the girls in your class swore they'd been kissed. I kissed you so you wouldn't be the odd one out."

In spite of herself, she laughed. "If I remember correctly, I threatened you with a ball bat if you didn't. You ran all the way to the arroyo."

"I made sure we were out of sight of this nosy bunch. I didn't want a critique of my first kiss." He pulled her close again. "But I'd like one now, if you don't mind."

She considered him a moment. "I'm thinking I need a couple more to compare, but I warn you…it will be hard to top the first two."

"Well, would you look at how cozy baby brother's getting with our little sister." Marcelo's mocking voice brought the rest of the family to the kitchen. Adele tried to pull away but Raoul tightened his arm across her shoulder as he turned to face his family. She felt a flush begin at the top of her head and race to consume her entire body.

"Honey, that didn't sound quite right." Kayla wrapped her arms around her husband's waist; a tiny giggle followed her words. "She can't be your little sister and Raoul your baby brother. That wouldn't be biblical."

"No," Marcelo drawled. "I guess until the wedding, we don't have a little brother anymore."

The room rocked with laughter. Adele couldn't help herself. She laughed in sheer joy. The family had chosen her. She knew in reality they would never turn their back on Raoul, but it felt good, even in teasing, to know that they considered her family and they loved her.

The back door slammed against the wall and her dad rushed in, his eyes wide and flashing like a wild man. "It's hailing golf balls outside. Tearing the trees all to pieces. And Oscar said the weatherman said a cold front is coming in."

Raoul tensed beside her. "This is ludicrous. This is September. How much of a cold front can there be this early in the season?"

"Adele, go check it out online. Raoul, the men are waiting on you to tell them what to do."

He opened the door and they could hear what they'd missed before. Large ice balls fell from the sky and the lawn already looked as if it had snowed. They gathered around the windows, amazed at the sight before them. Adele watched Raoul's face fall and shadows of fatigue lined his cheeks. This could destroy the winter harvest. Frantically she sought for a way to help. There was none until she remembered a Bible verse from Sunday school, "Call upon me in the day of trouble and I will deliver thee." Without any thought for how it would look or sound she blurted out, "Let's pray." All eyes were on her but she would not, could not, deny that urging. She knew it would work. She fell on her knees in front of the sofa, crying out loud, "Lord, please help us. He's worked so hard. Don't let it all be in vain. Please protect our harvest." Someone knelt beside her, gathered her close. She instinctively knew it was Raoul. She turned in his arms and held on tight. It was then she heard Juan Antonio take over her prayer.

Before Raoul could rise, she took his face in both hands and, looking him in the eye, she whispered the words on her heart. "Don't you dare give up. I don't care if every tree falls to the ground, I never want to see you defeated again. We will downsize, go smaller if we have to. Just don't walk away."

He pulled her tightly to him and stood up, taking her with him. "I promise I will never walk away again." He kissed the tip of her nose. Then he looked at his brothers. "Let's go see the damage."

Chapter 15

The men ran for their trucks. The hail had stopped but the damage was already done. Marcelo's new truck looked as if someone had shot it full of bullet holes. Thank the Lord, Raoul had parked his in the garage and it had escaped damage. Carina and Juan Antonio had parked near the veranda and her car had sustained only a few dents in the back fender. Adele followed Raoul to the garage, pulling on a long-sleeved shirt she'd grabbed passing through the laundry room. "Adele, you can't go."

"Please, Raoul. I will stay out of the way, but let me help. Please."

He could deny her nothing. Never had been able to, still couldn't. He climbed into the truck, relieved when she climbed in beside him. He knew the work they would have to do would be too hard for her, but she needed to be there and he liked it that she felt that way.

His men had gathered at the packing shed.

"Drag those tarps out of the back bin." Her dad issued orders as they approached. "Adele, see if you can find blankets or old sheets and get them to us as quickly as you can. What else do you need us to do, son?" Her dad looked to Raoul for direction. He was an accountant and business manager by trade and though he knew a bit of the growing side of the business, he had no clue how to prevent more damage.

Raoul turned to one of the men. "We'll need the heaters—all of them. And send someone for kerosene. We'll have to run them through the night."

Juan Antonio and Marcelo joined him, and Adele watched in awe as they took orders from their younger brother, never questioning him, but hurrying to comply. They piled the trucks high with the unusual assortment of coverings and as many heaters as the two trucks would haul. Moments later they arrived at the north fields where they had ten acres of young saplings.

"Give me a hand here, Adele." Raoul shook open a tarp and handed her one corner. They flipped it up into the air so that it opened full length but it covered only one of the trees. The futility of their actions sank heavily upon her chest. There was no way they could cover every tree in all these acres.

"There's no way this will work." She voiced her thoughts out loud.

"Have some faith, woman." He winked at her but the worry lines around his eyes increased. He drove a stake into one corner then into the ground. He slid the corner up the stake until Adele could stand under it. They did all four corners and when they finished, their tarp met the one her dad and Juan Antonio had put over the next tree. So, two tarps actually covered about five trees. The men worked in teams, driving stakes in the corners to keep the wind from blowing the tarps away.

Adele turned to look for something smaller she could work with on her own so Raoul would have stronger help. Stinging rain pelted her face, but she worked on through the evening. She lost Raoul in the crowd but every now and then she heard someone call his name so she knew he was nearby. She could not help but admire the beautiful young saplings, which would eventually grow into big grapefruit trees. The evidence was unmistakable: Raoul had worked long and hard to get this part of the orchard growing.

"Sweetheart, will you text Carina and ask her to go to the store and buy fifteen of the largest tarps she can find and to bring every spare blanket from the house?"

She turned to face him and her feet slid in the mud. He caught her around the waist and swept her against him. They were soaked to the skin. She wanted to snuggle against his warmth until the coldness seeped from her body. She settled for a kiss on his chin and started to walk away when he picked her up in his arms and carried her to shelter under one of the makeshift tents. Her arms around his neck, she kissed the side of his face. She liked having the liberty to do so. From the look in his eyes, he wasn't averse to it, either.

She walked back to the barn, placing a call to Carina, and then she asked Kayla to fix food and bring it to the packing shed.

In no time, it seemed, the girls arrived together, and Adele called her dad and told him to bring some of the men to eat. She planned to send them back with more tarps and blankets. She was afraid to drive her little car because it could easily get stuck in the mud.

Kayla had prepared taco soup and garlic bread. She'd brought the commercial coffeepot with her and proceeded to make several gallons of hot coffee. Adele fed the men in shifts because they couldn't afford for all of them to stop completely. Adele worked on through the night, doing whatever came to hand, and never thought about quitting.

At almost five the next morning, his men dragged into the packing shed. They looked haggard and were covered in mud, but they were in good spirits and had saved the baby trees. They later learned that the temperature never dropped below freezing, so the trees would have been okay without their hard work, but no one felt sorry for the precautions they'd taken. It had been a team effort and Raoul had never been so proud of Adele in his life. Raoul held the driver's-side door open and motioned her to get into the truck. She wearily climbed in, too tired to protest or go around to the other side on her own.

He climbed in and turned the key, waiting for the diesel to warm up before he cranked it. He put the truck in gear and pulled her close to his side under the curve of his arm. She curled into him and the feelings in his heart intensified. For the larger part of his life, she'd been a trouper. Joe had been right. She never gave up. She'd worked quietly in the background, competently carrying out the things he'd given her to do.

They drove the short distance to the hacienda and parked as it began to pour again. The rainy season had arrived in South Texas with a vengeance.

"Oh, law. Will this undo our hard work?" Her sleepy voice whispered along his nerve endings. He never wanted to be separated from her. He wanted her with him all the time. He dreaded going into the house because they'd have to separate and go to their individual rooms.

"No, babe. Only if we have a flash flood."

She curled her feet under her. "My feet are freezing."

Only then did he realize she wore flip-flops. "We need to get you into the house."

"No, please. Can we stay out here and talk? Are you too tired?"

He flipped the heat on high and pulled a towel from behind the seat. "My thoughts exactly." He removed her shoes and made her wrap her feet in the towel.

But she didn't say anything, just sat snuggled in his arms with her head on his shoulder, and he found himself unable to stop talking. The roles had for sure been reversed. "I'm so proud of you, sweetheart. You stayed right with me tonight. You didn't whine or cry or give up. We make a great team, don't you agree?"

"Yes, I agree."

"Just imagine, Della. We have made it through the tough years. Wonderful things are ahead for us. When we get through this harvest, I will have some time off. I'm not going to plant any more for two years. I will work and cultivate what we have and make sure the trees produce like they should. If not, I'll start the thinning out process.

"But we can go anywhere you'd like. Haven't you always wanted to go to Paris?" At her nod, he continued. "Then let's plan it. We need to take care of each other, nurture each other's desires and dreams, right?"

"Right."

"And I'm not sure I want strangers in my house. If we want to sleep in late, we can, without worrying about appointments. And if we want to sleep in different bedrooms each night, we can. It will be no one's business but our own. *Comprende?*"

"Si. Comprende."

"Things will start paying off, you'll see. I gave us back to God and the Bible says when a man's ways please the Lord, He makes even his enemies be at peace with him. So we will have bad times, I'm sure, but He will give us more peaceful times to make up for it."

He kissed the top of her head and she turned her face up like an eager little bird. He could no more resist that invitation than he could deny his next breath. Her lips were warm and sweet on his. The kiss sent the pit of his stomach into a funny whirl. He slammed the door on his thoughts and eased her out of his arms. She started to protest but his mouth swooped down to capture hers in a short, hard kiss. "I'm weak right now, sweetheart, and could get us into a lot of trouble. I don't want to do anything wrong. We will stay pure in the eyes of God and He will bless us for it." He took her flip-flops off the dash and handed them to her.

She looked at him as if he'd grown two heads. In fact, she looked like she had when they were kids and she'd held him down until he said uncle or agreed to whatever scheme she was up to at the time. The sun had just popped over the horizon and bathed the beauty of her face with a golden glow. She took his breath away.

"You've done a bucket load of talking this morning, Mr. Fuentes, but you've left one minor detail out."

Joy bells started ringing in his soul. Leave it to his Della to get straight to the point and want things in black and white. No gray areas for his girl. "Oh? What's that?"

"Are you asking me to marry you or not?"

He drew back in fake horror. "Are you crazy? I would never be stupid enough…" he stuttered. "How could you ever think I'd be foolish enough to ask you…before I asked your dad. He would kill us both."

She beat him with the flip-flops until he grabbed her around the waist, opened the door and almost fell out with her on top of him, her arms clasped wildly about his neck for support—right into the path of her dad who'd just walked from the north field because they'd forgotten him.

"I'm waiting."

Adele sat on the couch, watching in disbelief the scene unfolding in front of her. "Dad, I'm twenty-three years old, a few years past needing—"

"Be quiet, Adele."

"But this is ridiculous."

"I'm not talking to you, Adele, so you would be smarter to zip it."

"Joe, if…"

"That's 'sir,' to you."

Adele'd had enough. She stood up to leave but her dad stepped in front of her. She'd never seen this side of him. He pointed at the sofa and she sat back down.

"Joe…sir." Raoul actually seemed afraid of her dad and that blew her mind. Raoul had never been afraid of anybody. "I wish you would give me a chance to do this right. You're forcing my hand and that's what we'll always remember in the future. It will spoil an otherwise perfect story."

"Too bad, Raoul. When you messed with my daughter's reputation, you crossed the line. Now what is all this hashtagging about?"

Raoul looked at Adele with an apologetic grin. "I wanted to privately ask for your daughter's hand in marriage. Then I planned a special evening at Padre Island to propose. Now it's ruined."

"You shoulda thought about that before you started smooching in the truck."

"Joe, you know that's absurd. I always treat her with respect."

"Well…" Her dad folded his arms across his chest. "Get on with it."

"Dad, what are you doing? Have you gone mad?"

"Not another word, Adele."

She watched the play of emotions on Raoul's face. He hated being forced into anything.

He walked to her and sat on the coffee table, facing

her. He took her hands in his and shrugged his shoulders in mock resignation. "This is not how I wanted to do this, nor how I would have planned it, but only because I would have liked for you to have great memories of my proposal to you." He frowned at her dad who stood barely three feet from them. "But never doubt that this is what I want with my whole heart." He went down on one knee. "Will you marry me, beautiful Della, and finally put me out of my misery?"

Her dad handed him a ring. Raoul protested. "This is ridiculous. I will buy her a ring."

"You did. That one's from you."

They both looked at the ring and Adele gasped. It was the most beautiful ring she'd ever seen, and given the choice she'd have chosen it over any she had seen. "It was your mother's, Adele. I had the diamonds on the side added. They were from Marta's ring." Her dad seemed rather pleased with himself. She felt some of her angst leave.

Raoul slid the ring on her finger—a perfect fit. She put her arms around his shoulders and he stood, taking her with him, her feet leaving the floor. He turned his back on her dad, shielding her from his parental watchdogging. "I love you, Della."

"I love you, my handsome prince."

Suddenly Juan Antonio, Carina, Marcelo and Kayla entered from the foyer where they'd hidden until the deed was done. "Woo-hoo!" "Yeah." "That's what I'm talking about." Raoul took it well but Adele needed answers.

"Why did you all ruin the only proposal I'll ever receive?"

"Think about it, Adele," Carina explained. "What's the one thing Raoul tormented us all with when we needed someone to talk to or a shoulder to cry on? The advice he always gives?"

"Get over it or get therapy?"

At their nods and huge grins she became more flustered. "What does that have to do with him proposing marriage to me?"

Her dad explained. "For the rest of his life, if he complains about being forced to get married, we all can finally say, 'Get over it or get therapy.'"

Everyone started talking at once, the boys slapping Raoul on the back with congratulations and advice. She still wasn't satisfied with the explanation. "So, Dad, how did you get roped in to doing this?"

"I was the only one that could keep a straight face, and I got tired of watching the two of you botch things up. For goodness' sake, get married."

One thing her dad didn't say out loud but she caught loud and clear. Raoul hated forceful authority. Had he not wanted to marry her, this would have chased him away. You had better not try and force him to do anything; ask nicely and he'd do pretty much anything.

Her dad, though, in his own special way, had just provided assurance to his insecure child that she was loved and she would always know that Raoul wanted to marry her. She hugged her friends with thankfulness that God had once again answered her every need. But when she felt his arms surround her from behind, she leaned back against him; she had needed no proof from her dad. Raoul had asked her before her earthly father had forced him to. Her Heavenly Father knew better than anyone that she needed that assurance and He'd taken care of it much better than her earthly friends and family.

Raoul leaned down and whispered in her ear. "Should we tell them I asked you in the truck?"

She looked up at him and caught the devilish look in his eyes. She laughed happily. "Nah, it will be our secret—just yours and mine."

"I'll let you have four hours of sleep, and then you and I are driving to Padre Island and we're celebrating the right way. Then I'll finally get to tell you I love you and you can put me out of my misery by promising to devote the rest of your life to me." His breath against her ear made tiny shivers run up and down her spine. What a great, handsome, exciting man her childhood friend had grown up to be.

Exactly five hours later she sat in the beautiful restaurant of the Island Grand. Her stomach was too full of butterflies to eat more than a few bites. The white linen tablecloths against the black marble tables showcased the fine china, glassware and silverware. The lunch crowd had gone and only one other couple occupied a table on the other side. Their heads were bowed close as they talked in hushed tones to each other. Every few minutes, Raoul stole a kiss or he offered her bites of dessert off his fork.

"Can we get married soon?"

"How soon is soon to you?"

"Tomorrow is not soon enough for me, but I know you will want a church wedding, so I'm willing to wait, but please have mercy." He kissed the side of her ear, and she laid her face against his.

"But will you have time for a wedding and honeymoon since harvest starts next month?"

"Maybe not in Paris because when we go there, I would like to stay about a month, but a week in Cancun or the Bahamas would be a piece of cake."

"But, my handsome prince, there would be days of tux fittings and groomsmen gifts to buy, and what about bachelor parties and wedding showers? And pictures?"

"So you're saying we can't get married till January or February?" His beautiful eyes showed his disappointment.

She laughed at him. "That's three months, Raoul. We just became engaged this morning."

"Okay, but let's settle it right now so I will have something to sustain me through the dark lonely days ahead."

"You crazy man. I will be with you on those days."

He fingered the ring he'd placed on her hand in front of her dad. "Do you really like this ring? I will get you whichever one you want."

"I love this ring. And hopefully it didn't cost a war pension to have made."

"It didn't. Your dad presented me with the bill before we left the house. He said he felt it was my responsibility to pay for it." He chuckled. "Joe never changes."

"Can you believe we've come this far, Raoul? I love

you so much. I loved you as a boy, but the man you've become takes my breath away."

"I love you, too, my darling. I thank God every day that I have you in my life."

They drove back to the hacienda, her hand clasped in his. Every now and then he lifted it to his lips and they traded kisses once they were on the open road. She loved kisses. She felt she did a little better each time.

Chapter 16

The next months were filled with exactly what she'd described to Raoul. One thing she made sure of: the preparations did not come between them. Even though the finances of The Queen were stable again, they could crash in a moment. They were making it okay, but one blight of trees or a freeze would annihilate their fragile budget.

She, Carina, Kayla and Alma made decorations. She finally settled on a cake and Kayla wouldn't allow her to pay for it. She said it was her wedding gift. Carina brought her mother to the hacienda and the three of them cut and sewed a breathtakingly beautiful satin gown. The invitations were ordered and sent out and time flew by.

She and Raoul had gone ahead with the historical society and they brought a plaque to place beside the front door, explaining the age of the house and the builders. At the gatehouse they'd placed a huge bronze sign with small gold letters and a picture of the Fuentes ancestor who built The Queen. Their first tour had been last week. A group of senior citizens came up on a bus from Alamo, a neighboring town, and spent two hours over the allotted time slot, but they'd loved The Queen and the appreciation they'd shown for the old place had met a need inside her.

"Where's your list?"

Adele looked up at Carina and pointed. "Why?"

"We can mark off bridesmaid and matron dresses. Are you sure you can't talk your dad into renting a tux and walking you down the stairs?"

"I could. I just don't want to. I want him to be comfortable on my wedding day. His happiness is very important to me." She wished she remembered the man he was before her mother died.

"Okay, well, have you seen the stairs and foyer doors?"

At Carina's pleased expression, Adele jumped up and raced from the room. She slid in socks on the tile floor and came to a stop at the foot of the stairs. Her eyes widened and her breath caught in her throat. She simply stared, unable to say a word. Kayla's decorations had transformed the old but stately Hispanic hacienda into a magnificent showcase.

"Look at the doors."

Adele turned and her hands covered her mouth. Wreaths, almost the size of the ten-foot doors, were stunning in their beauty and design. "Kayla has more talent in her little finger than I have in my entire body."

"Kayla didn't make those, Alma did."

Adele's mouth dropped open. "Really?" At Carina's nod she said, "I knew Kayla left a lot of the work, even management, in Alma's hands. I just didn't know she could do that." She pointed at the stairs and doors.

"Juan Antonio told me you and Raoul have new plans for The Queen."

It had taken a while, but they had finally stopped the family meetings concerning the hacienda. Raoul had told them that while he appreciated all the help they'd given, from now on he and Adele would be making the decisions on which direction to take the hacienda.

"Yes, starting in June, we will be running a bed-and-breakfast two weekends out of the month. We have no intentions or need to do any more than that. The tours are booked on the weeks we have no guests. We're pretty excited."

"And your finances?" At Adele's inquiring look, Carina explained. "I'm not being nosy, truly. I know this wedding will cost more money than you originally wanted to spend and I was trying to decide our wedding gift."

"Finances are stable at the moment and Raoul will get a huge check from the Alaskans in the next week or so. That will carry us through the summer." She bit the string from the loop of the needle. She'd just sewn fifty rice bags. And could have kicked herself for not thinking of bubbles instead.

Raoul chose that moment to run in for a quick hug

and kiss. He tossed three magazines on the table in front of her, then grabbed a bunch of grapes from the bowl, tossing one at a time in the air and catching them in his mouth.

"Look at my handsome man, Carina. He's so talented."

"Pffftt, mine so has yours outdone. He can do that with popcorn." Adele couldn't control her burst of laughter.

"Well, if you're going to insult me, I'm outta here." He swung the bar stool around and placed Adele's arms around his shoulders. She loved being on the same eye level as he. "You better think lovely thoughts about me, woman. I'm out there slaving hard for you." She kissed the tip of his nose and then rubbed a hand gently under his chin. She loved the feel of his beard, though closely shaven, at this time of day it would be a bit prickly. He rubbed noses with her, his eyes never leaving hers, and then he turned to go. She reached for him, latching on to his shirt. "Get back here and give me a proper kiss." He didn't have to be asked twice and they sort of lost themselves until Carina cleared her throat.

He left Adele wishing she'd followed her heart and gone to the justice of the peace. They would be married by now, living their happily ever after.

"So, what are the house plans books for?"

If Adele hadn't known Carina to be the nicest person in the world, she'd have thought she might be the nosiest. "Raoul and I are thinking about building a home and moving out of The Queen."

"Oh?"

"Well, we've talked about it and if The Queen becomes self-supporting then that part of our money woes is over. But we want to be together, not tied to this place that robs us of so much personal time. Does that make sense?"

"Perfect. And I'm glad you've finally gotten to the place where you could give her up."

"Me, too." She added the last rice bag to the decorated basket and stretched her back. "I can't wait for the next two days to pass. I will be so thankful to finally become Mrs. Raoul Fuentes."

"Your wedding will be a dream come true?"

"I've dreamed of it since I was seven, so yes, marrying Raoul is a dream come true."

Two days later, she stood in front of the mirror, alone at last. She stared at the woman she'd become and thought of the long, difficult road she'd traveled to get to this day. She leaned in to get a better look, a close-up of the features she knew so well. But what she saw went far beyond her facial features made beautiful by perfectly applied makeup and curls tamed to sleek and precise styling. There was calm, peace, even serenity looking back at her.

And who would have thought the love of a good man could have done this for her. The ugliness of doubt, jealousy, fear, stubborn willfulness and even manipulation, had been replaced with happiness that shone on the face in the mirror. With complete trust in the man waiting downstairs. She closed her eyes and whispered a sincere thank-you to the Lord. The words of an old hymn ran through her mind. *Whatever my lot, Thou hast taught me to say, it is well, it is well with my soul.*

"No, Raoul. You can't go in there." Adele heard the door behind her open then shut just as quickly. Carina entered but held the door closed so Raoul couldn't. "It's bad luck to see the bride before the ceremony," she stated firmly.

"Let me in, Carina. I need to see her."

"Don't make me call your brothers, Raoul."

Adele moved around Carina to speak through the crack in the door. "What's up, my handsome prince?"

"It's taking too long." He paused and Adele blinked back tears.

"I feel the same."

"I miss you." He cleared the huskiness from his voice. "Can't we just get Pastor Jacobs to come up here and marry us and let the people celebrate without us?"

Adele pulled on the door, longing to comfort him, to share this moment with her heart's other part.

"Oh. No. You. Don't." Carina pushed the send button on her phone and stepped in front of Adele, effectively blocking the door. "Your brothers are on the way, Raoul. Go back downstairs. You only have fifteen more minutes to wait."

"Adele, give me your hand."

Adele gave Carina her fiercest don't-mess-with-me look, trying hard not to laugh out loud. Carina waved her hands in defeat but huffed her opposition. Adele placed her hand in Raoul's, her head close to the crack in the door. Tears filled her eyes as he began to pray.

How perfect. She had needed this to seal the love and honor she felt for him. This man God had given her.

Two seconds after his prayer ended, she heard Juan Antonio and Marcelo running up the stairs. Raoul kissed her hand, released it and met his brothers at the top as he started down.

"Hey, guys. What y'all doing up here? Aren't you supposed to be seating guests?"

Carina rolled her eyes and Adele burst out laughing.

"That man of yours is incorrigible." She took a tissue and wiped softly under Adele's eyes. "How dare he mess up my makeup job?"

Kayla and Alma whisked through the door, the cotton print, tea-length sundresses with matching jackets showing off their slender waistlines, and the floppy sunhats the contrast to their beautiful outfits. "I'm so nervous," Alma said.

"You?" Kayla asked incredulously. "How do you think Adele feels?"

All eyes turned to Adele. She held out a steady hand. "I'm calm as a cucumber."

"You look beautiful."

"Yes, you do. Lovely." Carina pulled the short veil over Adele's forehead. "Okay, let's begin this most blessed event." She, Kayla and Alma walked to the stairs and assumed their positions to go down single file. The music started softly. Alma first, then Kayla. Carina last. At the bottom of the stairs, Daniel offered his arm to escort Alma past the crowd gathered in the huge foyer. Then Kayla and Marcelo, Juan Antonio and Carina. It was four steps at the most to the stairs, but

Adele's heart pounded and she wondered for the umpteenth time if she could get down the stairs in this dress.
She arrived at the top and her dad stepped up beside her.
His hair styled, black tux and cummerbund to match
the girls' dresses, he was the most handsome Adele had
ever seen him.

"Dad?" Tears welled in her eyes.

"You didn't really think I'd let you make this trip
alone, now did you? My only child?"

He leaned forward and kissed her on the cheek.
Adele thought her heart might burst.

"Oh, Dad. My cup runneth over."

He took her hand, kissed it and placed it in the crook
of his arm. He looked down the stairs, then back at her.
"Ready?"

She took a deep breath, nodded and took the first
step. She looked up just in time to see Raoul walk across
and look up at her. Her knees began to tremble and she
tightened the hold on her dad's arm. Her heart lurched
madly. Then he captured her with his eyes and his love
circled her like a warm blanket. Her nervousness sub-
sided and she felt blissfully happy, fully alive.

On the last step, she was eye to eye with Raoul and
he accepted her hand from her dad. His eyes clung to
hers, analyzing her reaction, probing to her very soul.
The little boy she had given her heart to, had cared for
during sick days, would now care for her until death
parted them. She watched the play of emotions on his
face and knew her eyes mirrored the same. He leaned
forward and kissed her cheek.

Carina cleared her throat and the beginnings of a

smile tipped the corners of his mouth. He winked at Adele, then moved back, and she took the last step into the rest of their lives.

* * * * *

REQUEST YOUR FREE BOOKS!

2 FREE INSPIRATIONAL NOVELS
PLUS 2
FREE
MYSTERY GIFTS

Love Inspired

YES! Please send me 2 FREE Love Inspired® novels and my 2 FREE mystery gifts (gifts are worth about $10). After receiving them, if I don't wish to receive any more books, I can return the shipping statement marked "cancel." If I don't cancel, I will receive 6 brand-new novels every month and be billed just $4.74 per book in the U.S. or $5.24 per book in Canada. That's a savings of at least 21% off the cover price. It's quite a bargain! Shipping and handling is just 50¢ per book in the U.S. and 75¢ per book in Canada.* I understand that accepting the 2 free books and gifts places me under no obligation to buy anything. I can always return a shipment and cancel at any time. Even if I never buy another book, the two free books and gifts are mine to keep forever.

105/305 IDN F49N

Name	(PLEASE PRINT)	

Address		Apt. #

City	State/Prov.	Zip/Postal Code

Signature (if under 18, a parent or guardian must sign)

Mail to the **Harlequin® Reader Service:**
IN U.S.A.: P.O. Box 1867, Buffalo, NY 14240-1867
IN CANADA: P.O. Box 609, Fort Erie, Ontario L2A 5X3

**Are you a subscriber to Love Inspired books
and want to receive the larger-print edition?
Call 1-800-873-8635 or visit www.ReaderService.com.**

* Terms and prices subject to change without notice. Prices do not include applicable taxes. Sales tax applicable in N.Y. Canadian residents will be charged applicable taxes. Offer not valid in Quebec. This offer is limited to one order per household. Not valid for current subscribers to Love Inspired books. All orders subject to credit approval. Credit or debit balances in a customer's account(s) may be offset by any other outstanding balance owed by or to the customer. Please allow 4 to 6 weeks for delivery. Offer available while quantities last.

Your Privacy—The Harlequin® Reader Service is committed to protecting your privacy. Our Privacy Policy is available online at www.ReaderService.com or upon request from the Harlequin Reader Service.
We make a portion of our mailing list available to reputable third parties that offer products we believe may interest you. If you prefer that we not exchange your name with third parties, or if you wish to clarify or modify your communication preferences, please visit us at www.ReaderService.com/consumerchoice or write to us at Harlequin Reader Service Preference Service, P.O. Box 9062, Buffalo, NY 14269. Include your complete name and address.

LIDIR13R

REQUEST YOUR FREE BOOKS!

2 FREE INSPIRATIONAL NOVELS
PLUS 2
FREE
MYSTERY GIFTS

Love Inspired
HISTORICAL
INSPIRATIONAL HISTORICAL ROMANCE

YES! Please send me 2 FREE Love Inspired® Historical novels and my 2 FREE mystery gifts (gifts are worth about $10). After receiving them, if I don't wish to receive any more books, I can return the shipping statement marked "cancel." If I don't cancel, I will receive 4 brand-new novels every month and be billed just $4.74 per book in the U.S. or $5.24 per book in Canada. That's a savings of at least 21% off the cover price. It's quite a bargain! Shipping and handling is just 50¢ per book in the U.S. and 75¢ per book in Canada.* I understand that accepting the 2 free books and gifts places me under no obligation to buy anything. I can always return a shipment and cancel at any time. Even if I never buy another book, the two free books and gifts are mine to keep forever.

102/302 IDN F5CY

Name	(PLEASE PRINT)	
Address		Apt. #
City	State/Prov.	Zip/Postal Code

Signature (if under 18, a parent or guardian must sign)

Mail to the Harlequin® Reader Service:
IN U.S.A.: P.O. Box 1867, Buffalo, NY 14240-1867
IN CANADA: P.O. Box 609, Fort Erie, Ontario L2A 5X3

Want to try two free books from another series?
Call 1-800-873-8635 or visit www.ReaderService.com.

* Terms and prices subject to change without notice. Prices do not include applicable taxes. Sales tax applicable in N.Y. Canadian residents will be charged applicable taxes. Offer not valid in Quebec. This offer is limited to one order per household. Not valid for current subscribers to Love Inspired Historical books. All orders subject to credit approval. Credit or debit balances in a customer's account(s) may be offset by any other outstanding balance owed by or to the customer. Please allow 4 to 6 weeks for delivery. Offer available while quantities last.

Your Privacy—The Harlequin® Reader Service is committed to protecting your privacy. Our Privacy Policy is available online at www.ReaderService.com or upon request from the Harlequin Reader Service.

We make a portion of our mailing list available to reputable third parties that offer products we believe may interest you. If you prefer that we not exchange your name with third parties, or if you wish to clarify or modify your communication preferences, please visit us at www.ReaderService.com/consumerschoice or write to us at Harlequin Reader Service Preference Service, P.O. Box 9062, Buffalo, NY 14269. Include your complete name and address.

LIHDIR13R

ReaderService.com

Manage your account online!

- Review your order history
- Manage your payments
- Update your address

*We've designed
the Harlequin® Reader Service
website just for you.*

Enjoy all the features!

- Reader excerpts from any series
- Respond to mailings and special monthly offers
- Discover new series available to you
- Browse the Bonus Bucks catalog
- Share your feedback

Visit us at:
ReaderService.com